Whispering Hope

Other Books in the Keystone Stables Series

Whispering Hope

BOOK 7

KEYSTONE
Stables

..... *Marsha Hubler* .....

ZONDER**kidz**

ZONDERVAN.com/
AUTHORTRACKER
follow your favorite authors

We want to hear from you. Please send your comments
about this book to us in care of zreview@zondervan.com. Thank you.

ZONDERKIDZ

Whispering Hope
Copyright © 2009 by Marsha Hubler

Requests for information should be addressed to:
Zonderkidz, *Grand Rapids, MI* 49530

Library of Congress Cataloging-in-Publication Data

Hubler, Marsha, 1947-
    Whispering hope / by Marsha Hubler.
        p. cm. — (Keystone Stables ; bk. 7)
        Summary: When a wild pinto mustang, Rebel, and an equally wild new foster
girl, Wanda, arrive at Keystone Stables, Skye feels God urging her to reach out
and help them, whether they want her to or not.
        ISBN 978-0-310-71691-4 (softcover)
        [1. Behavior—Fiction. 2. Wild horses—Fiction. 3. Horses—Training—Fiction.
4. Christian life—Fiction. 5. Foster home care—Fiction.] I. Title.
        PZ7.H86325   Whi 2010
        [Fic]—dc22   4650 2398 8/11   2009023909

Interior illustrator: Lyn Boyer
Interior design and composition: Carlos Estrada and Sherri L. Hoffman

Printed in the United States of America

10 11 12 13 14 15 16 /DCI/ 23 22 21 20 19 18 17 16 15 14 13 12 11 10 9 8 7 6 5 4 3 2

❊❊❊

In memory of my father Joe,
who taught me the game of pool.

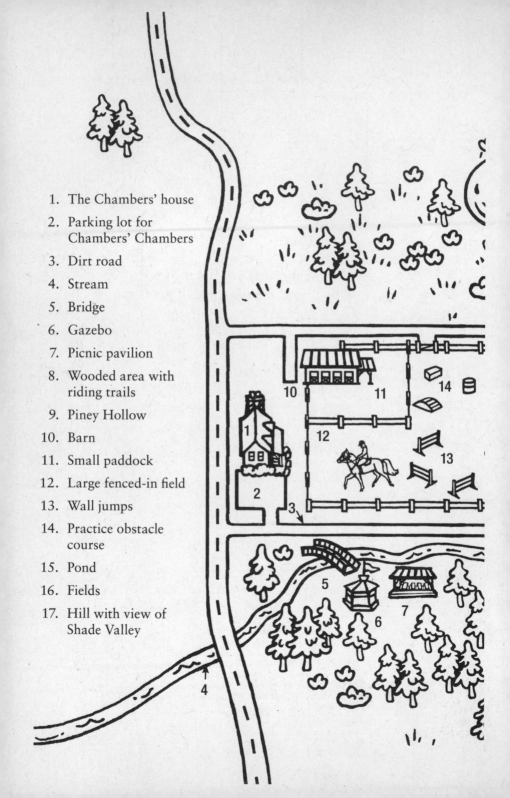

1. The Chambers' house
2. Parking lot for Chambers' Chambers
3. Dirt road
4. Stream
5. Bridge
6. Gazebo
7. Picnic pavilion
8. Wooded area with riding trails
9. Piney Hollow
10. Barn
11. Small paddock
12. Large fenced-in field
13. Wall jumps
14. Practice obstacle course
15. Pond
16. Fields
17. Hill with view of Shade Valley

Map of the Chambers' Ranch

Champ, you're eating like a hog today!" Thirteen-year-old Skye Nicholson smiled as she stroked her sorrel Quarter Horse's muzzle in a stall in the exhibitors' barn. She and her foster family were spending the last three days of February at the State Horse Show and Expo in Harrisburg, Pennsylvania. "Hold your horses and I'll get you some more hay."

Champ nickered and snuggled his nose against Skye's suede western vest.

"Will you get Diamond an extra section?" Morgan Hendricks, Skye's fifteen-year-old foster sister, yelled from the next stall where she sat in her wheelchair grooming her bay mare. "Diamond worked up a good sweat in our last class. Of course, she's eating for two, so she deserves another serving."

"No problem," Skye yelled back.

"Sometimes it pays to have cerebral palsy," Morgan kidded. "Other people get to do the hard work."

"Caring for horses is not hard work in my book!" Skye said, heading down a long corridor sandwiched between two rows of stalls that buzzed with horse business. She weaved in and out among riders primping their mounts until she reached the corner of the barn. All along the way, she relived the last few wonderful days at the horse show. *Second place in Junior Western Pleasure for Champ and me and third for Morgan and Diamond in the Special-Needs Halter Class. Not bad. Not bad at all!* At the end of the hallway, she opened the Dutch door to a dimly lit room filled with stacked hay bales. She walked to the stack, and as she reached and pulled down a hay bale, something moved behind the piles, forcing her to jump back.

Must be another stray cat, she thought as she stretched to look behind the bales. *What if she just had kittens? I bet she's hungry.*

Skye shifted a few bales to her left to see farther into the corner. "Whoa!" she yelped.

The glinting blade of a jackknife pointed directly at Skye.

In the dim light, Skye strained to study a thin figure holding the knife. His face in the shadow of a black baseball cap, visor cocked to the side, the stranger wore a washed-out jacket and soiled and tattered cargo pants. The right arm of the jacket bore a neon orange patch with the barely legible word "Blades."

Skye sized the intruder, started to back away, and opened her mouth, but no words came out. For the first time in her life, she was scared down to her toenails.

"Get lost, horse breath!" the stranger ordered. "You're on my turf now!"

Riveted to the floor, Skye again tried to speak. "I—I was only getting some hay for my horse."

"I said get lost!" he yelled as he poked the knife toward Skye.

Skye quickly analyzed the situation and decided she was no pushover with kids like this. She had run with this kind a long time ago, before she went to live at Keystone

Stables. In fact, she had *been* a kid like this. Skye's brown eyes flashed as she raked her hands through her long, dark hair. *Should I take on this skinny rail of a kid or not? Better not*, she reasoned. *Not with that knife pointing my way.*

In a flash, Skye turned and ran out the doorway and yelled to anyone who would listen. "Hey, there's a kid with a knife in this room!"

Every horseman within earshot stopped dead in his tracks and stared at Skye.

"A knife?" one girl yelled as she clutched her horse's halter.

"Call security!" a woman in English riding clothes and mounted on a black horse yelled as she reined her mount in the opposite direction.

Across the hall, a muscular man in Western attire and a ten-gallon hat came charging out of stall. With a pitchfork pointed in Skye's direction, he yelled, "Where is he? I'll take care of him."

As Skye focused down the long corridor toward the other end of the barn, she spotted Mr. and Mrs. Chambers standing in front of Champ's stall.

"Mom! Dad!" Skye yelled her lungs out. "There's a kid with a knife in the hay room!"

The man with the pitchfork charged across the hall. "Get out of the way, kid. I'm going in after him!"

"Skye, get away from there!" Mr. Chambers' voice echoed down the hallway as he ran toward Skye. "Eileen, call security, and I'll go check it out!"

Skye took several steps away from the door, and before the cowboy and his pitchfork reached the room, the intruder tore past Skye, the knife nowhere in sight. He took off full speed ahead, weaving around gawking contestants and jittery horses toward the open doorway at the other end of the barn.

"Hey!" Skye yelled, and took off after him.

"Skye, be careful!" Mr. Chambers yelled, running toward the kid.

"I can handle this joker!" *We'll just see how tough this bean pole is without his knife,* Skye thought as she picked up speed.

"Give it up, kid!" Mr. Chambers yelled, barreling down the hallway.

Just a breath behind the kid, Skye took a running leap and wrapped her arms around his legs. Falling flat on his chest, he squirted out an "Oomph," followed by a string of foul language.

With all her strength, Skye wrestled the stranger, pinning him face down. "I've got him!" Skye yelled as she spotted a bulge in the back pocket of his pants and retrieved the knife. At the same time, the cowboy and Mr. Chambers grabbed the boy by his arms. "Skye, let go," Mr. Chambers said. "We've got him."

Skye released her grip, and Mr. Chambers pulled the kid up to his feet.

"Let me go, you scuzzball!" Taking vicious swings at Mr. Chambers and the other man, the kid's cap went flying.

Skye scrambled to her feet, ready to throw her own punch.

"It's—it's a girl!" Skye said, gasping to catch her breath.

Spectators on both sides of the hall gawked and tried to calm their spooked horses.

"Let me go," the kid yelled. "I ain't done nothin'."

"Then what'cha runnin' for?" the cowboy asked with a firm grip on her arm.

A policeman came running down the hall with Mrs. Chambers trailing right behind and Morgan not far behind.

"All right, that's enough!" The policeman huffed in short breaths, grabbing hold of the girl, who kicked and tried to shake him off. "What's going on here?"

Mr. Chambers and the cowboy released their grip, and the cowboy backed away. "Looks like you got this case sewn up," the cowboy said as he left.

"Thanks for your help," Mr. Chambers huffed, raising his hand.

"Kid, I'm telling you to calm down right now," the officer ordered as he scuffled with the girl, "or I'm going to cuff you."

Cuffs with your hands behind your back are not fun, Skye remembered as she watched the kid reluctantly give in to the policeman's demands. Gasping for breath, Skye handed the knife to the officer. "He—I mean she—pulled this on me in the feed stall. I don't even know who she is."

"Wanda," the officer said, catching his own breath, "I thought I told you to stay clear of this place." He turned and shouted to the mesmerized crowd. "Everything's okay, folks. We've got everything under control. Go about your business."

With that, the spectators quickly returned to their hustle and bustle.

"Skye, are you all right?" Mrs. Chambers huffed, blue eyes flashing from under her beige Stetson.

"Yeah, I'm fine." Skye released a devilish smile as she brushed off her jeans. "It's been awhile since anyone pulled a knife on me. Just like old times!"

"Horse breath," Wanda snapped, scowling at Skye.

Skye studied the semblance of a boy and determined that if Wanda's chopped-off wavy brown hair were longer—and clean—and she'd gain a few pounds, she would be almost pretty, especially with her dark brown eyes and long eyelashes.

"What's happening?" Morgan said, parking her wheelchair next to Mr. Chambers. Her freckled face radiated red almost as much as her long kinky hair.

"Folks, I'm sorry about this," the officer said. "We've had trouble with two gangs in this part of town. They're always having turf wars that include this complex. Wanda here runs with the Blades from the south side. The Scorpions *think* they control the west side. Somehow, they both claim this territory as theirs. Wanda was probably on a graffiti binge tonight and had some interference from the enemy. Isn't that right, Wanda?"

Wanda pulled her arm free from the officer and picked up her cap. She yanked it down on her head, folded her arms, and said nothing. All the while, her eyes scanned the scene as if searching for someone.

Who's she looking for? Skye thought.

"Wanda, that expression on your face means only one thing," the officer said. "You've got some Scorpions hot on your trail, don'tcha?"

Wanda lowered her head and said nothing.

"Well, they won't find you tonight, not where you're going."

"Juvie hall," Skye said.

"That's right, young lady," the officer said. "She'll be safe there until she sees the judge — again. This time she'll be sent up. She has a record as long as a flagpole."

Mr. Chambers quickly squared his tan Stetson and extended his hand to the officer. "I'm Tom Chambers. This is my wife, Eileen, and these are my two foster daughters, Skye Nicholson and Morgan Hendricks."

Wanda looked up with a scowl and stared at Skye. "Whoop-dee-doo," she slurred.

"Wanda, just be quiet," the officer said as he shook Mr. Chambers' hand. "Officer Bill Connors, third precinct. This is *my* turf when the horse show is being held."

Wanda just folded her arms and scowled.

Mr. Chambers smoothed his brown mustache and released a friendly smile. "Officer, we own Keystone Stables, a special-needs dude ranch and foster-care facility about an hour north of here. My wife is also a special-needs therapist at the Maranatha Treatment Center near our ranch. Our lives are dedicated to helping salvage the youth of today that are so—well—I wonder if this young lady would like to spend a year at our place, away from the Scorpions." He directed his last words right at Wanda.

"There's always room for another kid at Keystone Stables!" Skye said, staring at the girl.

"I ain't in need of no 'salvaging,'" Wanda declared. "Me and my gram get along just fine."

"Sure you do," Officer Connors said. "The last time I talked to your grandmother, she said you hadn't been home nor in school for two weeks. Hanging out with that gang spells nothing but trouble with a capital T."

Mrs. Chambers smiled and reached out to shake Wanda's hand. Wanda just stared and scowled.

"Wanda," Mrs. Chambers said, "I'm very glad to meet you. I'd love if you'd consider spending some time with us. It's not that bad. We have horses and two dogs, and a game room, and a pool table, and—"

"A pool table?" Wanda looked up, and, although the girl made no attempt to shake hands, Skye thought her eyes betrayed a sudden interest.

"Yeah," Skye said. "My friend Chad, who's in our youth group at church, is showing me how to shoot pool."

"A lot of kids in the youth group like to shoot pool," Morgan said. "They're always hanging out at our place."

"Now you've got her attention," Officer Connors said. "Whenever I want to find Wanda, all I need to do is go to Joe's Billiard Room on Fifth Street. If she's not with the gang, she's usually hanging out there. She's a regular pool shark. Has her own stick and everything."

"You'd really like it at the ranch," Morgan said. "There's lots to do with the horses."

"I hate animals," Wanda said, "especially horses."

Then you'll hate Keystone Stables, Skye reasoned.

"I think you'd like them if you spent some time with them," Mr. Chambers said.

Officer Connors slipped the knife in his shirt pocket and squared his hat. "Well, folks, if you really want this kid, you're looking at a two month wait until the court schedule opens up to adjudicate her into your care. But that will give you time to put bars on all your windows." He chuckled.

"Very funny," Wanda sneered.

"I know a quicker way," Mrs. Chambers said. "If Wanda agrees to come, we can have papers drawn up immediately that her grandmother can sign to release her into our custody. We do it all the time when family members are involved."

Wanda stood in silence, pretending not to listen. Then she scowled in Skye's direction. "I ain't goin' no place where Horsebreath lives."

Skye found herself with mixed emotions. As a Christian, she knew that with God's help she and her foster family could give Wanda a second chance in life. Yet she wasn't sure about this tough gangbanger who could turn everything upside down in everybody's life. *I don't know if I can take a whole year of insults,* Skye thought. *But then, God changed me, so he can change anybody!*

"Mr. Chambers, if you can get permission from her grandmother, that'll work," Officer Connors said. "What I can do for all of you is take you to see Wanda's grandma as soon as possible. Wanda, is she home?"

Wanda just shrugged.

"What's your phone number?" he asked.

"None of your business," Wanda snapped.

"Miss Smart Aleck, you deserve a year's worth of shoveling horse manure. That will be better for you than any juvie hall or residential treatment facility I know." Officer Connors punched numbers into his cell phone. "I'll call headquarters and get the phone number. How long are you folks staying in town?"

"We were going to leave this evening, but we'll change our plans if we need to," Mr. Chambers said.

"With any luck, you can meet Wanda's next of kin tonight and get the process moving. In the meantime, Wanda will be spending a little time downtown."

Wanda shot another sour look at Skye, more hateful than the last. "Horse breath," she growled.

Skye gave Wanda a forced smile and sent up a quick prayer. *God, I'm going to need you big time with this one.*

chapter two

It was a bitterly cold Saturday in March, exactly a month to the day that Wanda had caused so much trouble at the horse show. Now Skye was coming to grips with the fact that for the next year she would have a new foster sister.

"When are Mom and Morgan getting here with Wanda?" Skye stirred a huge bowl of macaroni salad in the kitchenette next to the game room in the basement.

Mr. Chambers, standing beside Skye, had a large pot of beef barbecue bubbling on the stove. He glanced at the clock on the wall. "Well, let's see. They left at eight this morning to pick up Wanda at her grandmother's. An hour down, an hour to pack the car and say goodbye, and another hour back. They should be here any minute." He adjusted his towering chef's hat, which he always wore just for fun, and stirred the steaming hot food. "I hope the youth group gets here before they do."

"Me too," Skye said. "I think your idea to have Wanda meet the Youth for Truth kids from church is a great idea. Although it's going to be tough sharing Keystone Stables, you and Mom, and the pool table, and practically every-thing else but my toothbrush with this kid, I know that's

18

what God would want. All Wanda's known for years is gang life and running the streets. I bet she doesn't have one single friend in the whole wide world. Gangbangers will turn on you in a sneeze to save their own hide. I have a feeling she's already found that out. I sure found out the hard way. Been there. Done that."

"New friends would certainly help her think in a different way. And Christians are the best kind of friends. They're usually there for you when you're hurting," Mr. Chambers said.

Skye grabbed a pack of paper plates and started to stack them on the serving counter.

Knock! Knock! Knock! The outside door to the basement rattled, accompanied by a barrage of squeals and laughter.

"Hey, Tom, are you in there?" a familiar voice yelled from outside.

"Oh, good. The kids are here," Mr. Chambers said then yelled, "C'mon in, George!"

Mr. Chambers swept off his chef's hat and hurried to let in the crowd. Before he got there, the door flew open and a herd of about a dozen giggling, laughing, and talking-too-loud teens invaded the game room. After they greeted Mr. Chambers and Skye, they targeted the ping-pong table, three computers loaded with video games, and the pool table. In seconds, the place buzzed with explosive teen energy.

Skye slowed her kitchen duty to a snail's pace while she examined every face that rushed inside. *Where is he?* she wondered.

Her glance shifted to the doorway where the last teen, Chad Dressler, hurried in carrying his guitar. His curly blonde eyelashes and chipmunk smile immediately lit up the whole universe as far as Skye was concerned, and her heart started to pound like a bass drum. When Chad saw Skye, he made a beeline to the serving counter.

"Hey, Skye, what's up?" He whipped his guitar in place and strummed like he was introducing the next act in a vaudeville show. "Ta-dah!" he said. "So tell me about this new kid from Harrisburg. Her name's Wanda?"

As usual, Skye felt her face flush hot, but it wasn't from working in a busy kitchen. She stared into Chad's eyes and, suddenly, her knees felt like marshmallows. She glanced away and went back to setting out piles and piles of paper plates.

"Yeah, her name's Wanda Stallord," Skye said, "and she's one piece of work. She's in a gang. When we met with her and her grandmother two weeks ago to sign some papers, Wanda made it perfectly clear that she only agreed to come here because of that." Skye pointed to the pool table encircled by half a dozen teens. "But I know her kind. I think she's running scared—maybe from the rival gang—maybe from some of her own gang. You always have to be watching your back with that kind of life."

"Hmm." Chad rubbed his chin and gave Skye another heart-melting smile. "Seems to me that it wasn't that long ago that someone else in this house was as mean and cantankerous as Wanda. Do you remember who that was?"

Again, Skye felt her face heat up. She spun around, opened the refrigerator, and pulled out a twenty-four pack of soda.

"Here, let me help you with that." Chad put down his guitar and reached across the counter. He retrieved the box from Skye and started to rip the cardboard open. "So, Skye," he said with a chuckle, "do you remember that nasty kid who came here a while back? Huh?"

Skye looked into his eyes and decided right then and there, at that very moment, she would tell Chad anything, everything, he ever wanted to know about her rotten past. The trouble was that he already knew it. "Oh, all right, Chad Dressler, you know it was me. I thought you wanted to know about our new girl in boys' clothing?"

"Sure. Tell me more."

"Wanda told us that she wants to be a professional pool player when she's older. She also made it clear that she hates animals, especially horses, which kinda thrills me to all get out. I don't have to worry about her messing with Champ."

Mr. Chambers walked behind the counter, recovered his chef's hat, and started stirring his pot again. "How are you doing, Chad, and how's your job at Jacob's Hardware?"

"Great, Mr. C.," Chad said, pulling the soda cans out of the box and lining them up on the corner of the counter. "Most of the money from the twenty hours I work each week goes right into my college fund." His glance shifted from Mr. Chambers back to Skye. "So, what else do you know about this Wanda person?"

"She also made it clear that she doesn't believe in God," Skye said, stacking a pile of plastic forks near the plates. "In fact, she said she's not sure he even exists because she never saw him do anything for her in her life. That's really sad. She's in bad shape."

"Well, we've seen the Lord do miracles in other kids' lives here at Keystone Stables." Mr. Chambers winked at Skye. "With lots of prayer and tough love, I think God can change Wanda."

"I believe it can happen," Chad added, staring at Skye. "Why, look at this beautiful young lady here. You have a prime example of how God can change someone."

Fiery hot, Skye grabbed a bag of potato chips, popped it open, and dumped half the chips in a big plastic serving dish and the other half all over the counter. "Oops," she said as she scooped the strays back in the dish. Chad grabbed a few for himself and just laughed.

The basement door opened again, and this time Wanda Stallord came barging in like some dark princess claiming the rights to a newly conquered kingdom.

21

Wearing exactly the same clothes that she had on a month ago, she carried a black backpack slung over her shoulder and a small, thin black leather case in her right hand. Trailing behind her, Mrs. Chambers carried a small black overnight bag. Morgan wheeled in through the doorway with a brown paper bag on her lap.

"Wow!" Chad whispered. "She sure travels light."

Skye leaned forward on the counter top. "You don't need much more than a jackknife when you run with a gang," she whispered.

"And I know what's in that little case," Chad said as he leaned toward Skye. "Probably a two-hundred-dollar pool stick that she lifted."

"All right, you two," Mr. Chambers said. "Let's give her a chance."

Looking at Mr. Chambers, Skye giggled. "If she's half the trouble I was, you and Mom will probably retire from the kid salvaging business and raise guinea pigs."

Mr. Chambers let out a roll of laughter that made Skye giggle some more. "Now that's a good one. Guinea pigs indeed."

Skye glanced at Mrs. Chambers, who unzipped her coat, took a deep breath, and got everyone's attention. "Hey, kids, this is Wanda Stallord, our new foster daughter."

"Hi, Wanda!" the kids said.

"What's up?" Chad yelled.

"Welcome." George walked toward Wanda and extended his hand. "I'm George Salem, the kids' youth leader at church. We'll introduce everyone after we eat, right Tom?" George looked Mr. Chambers' way.

"Good idea, because the food's all ready," Mr. Chambers said. "All we need to do is pray and we can eat. We've got barbecue, chips, macaroni salad, and soda."

Mrs. Chambers reached for a plastic container on the counter. "And here are handi-wipes," she said. "You know I'm a cleany, but it's flu season, and I don't want anyone getting sick."

While the teens started forming a food line, Skye kept her eye on Wanda, who headed straight for the pool table.

Wanda shed her backpack, retrieved the pool stick from the case, and screwed the two parts together. She pulled a five-dollar bill from her pants pocket and flipped it on the table. "Double or nothing," she said. "Who's the best pool player here? I'll take him on in a game of Nine Ball, ball in hand on a foul."

"Chad's the best pool player," Marty, one of the teen boys, said.

"Yeah, Chad is," all the rest agreed.

"So where's Chad?" Wanda said.

"Right here." Chad sauntered to the table. "But let's eat first, okay?"

"Whoa!" Wanda said, giving Chad the once-over from head to toe. She poked back her cap, forcing the visor off her forehead. Her chopped-off bangs stuck out like burnt straw. "Well, well, well, what do we have here? A pretty boy. Get your stick, dreamboy."

"After we eat." Chad's flushing red cheeks were a telltale sign of his total embarrassment.

As Skye eyed the scene, she felt her own face turn red hot, but from anger.

Mr. Chambers stepped into the center of the room. "Let's pray and eat, and then we'll have the pool match."

Skye stared at Wanda with a new kind of interest. *She's not here even five minutes, and she's making trouble already. She better keep her paws off of him and just stick to shooting pool,* Skye fumed.

chapter three

S kye dropped her pencil on the dining room table, covered her face with her hands, and moaned. "I've only got two days left to finish this report for history class."

At home a few evenings after Wanda arrived, Skye sat doing her homework at the dining room table with Morgan and Wanda. Near the sliding glass door lay two West Highland terriers, the Keystone Stables mascots.

In the adjoining kitchen, Mrs. Chambers had busied herself with one of her favorite pastimes—cooking. The whole house smelled like an Italian restaurant.

Morgan worked on a page of algebra problems while Wanda was entertaining herself drawing a picture of a pool table on a scrap of paper. Every now and then, she threw a glance of disdain in Skye's direction and then at the dogs, Tippy and Tyler, who showed no interest in Wanda whatsoever.

While Skye did her homework, she studied her new foster sister out of the corner of her eye. Wanda's attitude and whole outlook on life made Skye reflect on her own past, remembering the time when she hated church—and God too.

Then there was the disaster last Sunday when Wanda made her grand entrance at church. Although most of the kids tried to make her feel welcome in the Youth for Truth Sunday school class, she slumped into a folding chair with her Blades jacket on and her feet propped up on a chair, sulking the whole time.

Skye knew that since Wanda had arrived, she was *the* hot topic with the youth group. Her skill with the pool stick at Keystone Stables had backed everyone into a corner, including Chad. Of course, the discussion about her acting so much like a boy took precedence with Hannah Gilbert and her new friend Beth Feaster, but only when Wanda's back was turned. *I know how they can be with their mouths*, Skye remembered. *I hope they stay clear of Wanda, or they might be limping around with two black eyes.*

"Mr. Welch said we're having a big unit test tomorrow." Morgan focused completely on her book. "This one will cover slopes and x/y intercepts and all that graphing stuff."

"I'm sure you'll ace it as usual." Skye said, then glanced at Wanda who had just slumped in her chair, folded her arms, and hung on her super scowl. Although Wanda had *finally* changed into a dark green sweatshirt and faded jeans, she still wore her ball cap cocked to one side and to the best of her ability portrayed "tough."

"Girls," Mrs. Chambers said from the kitchen, "You have about ten more minutes at the table. Then we'll need to set it for supper."

"Okay, Mom," Skye said.

Skye glanced at Morgan, then at Wanda. "Wanda, don't you have any homework?"

"I never have homework," she sassed.

Mrs. Chambers came to the table and sat next to Wanda. "Since you're not going to Madison Middle until next August, how about explaining your new school program to the girls."

"I'm going to do something weird called homeschooling. I'd rather do that than be stuck in the dumb class at school. But I'd rather shovel a ton of horse manure than do any books at all!" Wanda said.

"Wanda, I think you'll enjoy homeschooling and you'll learn a lot." Mrs. Chambers gave Wanda a warm smile.

Skye also smiled, hoping in vain to get the slightest hint of one in return. "C'mon, Wanda, tell us what you're doing. All I know is that you're homeschooling, and I don't know much about that."

"Me neither," Morgan said. "A few kids in our youth group homeschool, and they seem to be on the ball. But I'm not sure how that works. Tell us about it."

"What you don't know won't hurt you," Wanda snapped, and went back to her doodling.

"Aw, c'mon, Wanda," Mrs. Chambers said. "I'll help you explain it."

"There's nothing to tell." Pointing her skinny thumb at Mrs. Chambers, Wanda refused to look up. "I just suffer through my books with her during the day at the treatment center while she tries to crack some other nutcases."

"Wanda, they're not nutcases," Mrs. Chambers said, her eyes glancing around the table, "and neither are you. And there's a little more to homeschooling than that. We review her lessons every day and do homework and tests. Occasionally, she has a little bit of homework, like tonight. She has one English paper to do. She'll actually get a report card at the end of the year and take an achievement test to check her progress."

Skye twiddled her pencil in her fingers and looked at Wanda with great interest. "Well, do you think homeschooling will work for you?"

"Nothing will work for me because I'm stupid!" Wanda practically yelled and her cheeks turned fiery red.

Skye's nerves jumped and Morgan recoiled like Wanda had slapped her in the face.

"Wanda, you are *not* stupid." Mrs. Chambers touched Wanda's shoulder, but Wanda shrugged her off and kept staring at the table.

Mrs. Chambers continued. "Because you haven't gone to school much this year, you would have been lost in the eighth grade at Madison. I believe with a few months of review with me, you'll be ready to go there in the fall."

"Yeah, probably as a third grader," Wanda grumbled.

Skye forced a chuckle to try to lighten the mood. "So, you don't have homework to do now?"

"Oh, she has a little to do every night," Mrs. Chambers said. "But most of it is done during the day."

Wanda adjusted her cap visor dead center over her eyes. "I have a lot of choices sitting at Maranatha all day long. I can either do schoolwork or count the cracks in the walls of her office."

Everyone laughed but Wanda.

"She also has individual counseling and group therapy," Mrs. Chambers said. "You girls remember those days, don't you?"

"Oh, yes," Morgan said with a chuckle.

"Back then I wanted to forget them," Skye said, "but now I can see how much they helped me."

Wanda completely detached herself from the conversation. "Can I shoot some pool?" she asked Mrs. Chambers.

"Yes," Mrs. Chambers answered.

Just as Wanda launched out of her chair and headed away from the table, Mrs. Chambers stuck out her hand and, in one slick motion, caught Wanda by the sleeve. "Not so fast, young lady. You have a few things to do first."

Skye's glance met Morgan's as they both waited to see what would happen next. *Wanda finally met her match,* Skye mused. *When Mom says "young lady," she means business! I wish I could spare her the pain of what's coming if she doesn't listen!*

Wanda flopped her skinny frame back in the chair and stared pitchforks at Mrs. Chambers. "What!" she growled.

Mrs. Chambers gave Wanda her warmest smile and took a deep breath.

Uh-oh, Skye thought.

Mrs. Chambers held up her hands and touched her index finger. "First, I want you to finish that English paper about nouns and verbs."

Wanda slumped deep into the chair, folded her arms, and pursed her lips.

Mrs. Chambers then held up two fingers. "Secondly, and this will be after we eat supper and you've helped with the dishes, I'd like you to show the girls your newly decorated bedroom. No one has seen it since we went shopping on Saturday night and you picked out those new curtains and spread."

Wanda didn't move a muscle.

"Young lady, look at me when I speak to you," Mrs. Chambers demanded.

Skye's and Morgan's eyes widened as they traded uh-oh glances.

Wanda didn't move a muscle.

That girl's digging her own grave, Skye thought. "Wanda—"

"Girls," Mrs. Chambers spoke calmly to Skye and Morgan, "please leave us alone for a few minutes. I'll call you when I need help with supper."

"Yes, ma'am," Morgan said, backing her wheelchair away from the table.

"Yes, ma'am," Skye said, standing.

As she and Morgan headed down the hallway to their rooms, Skye couldn't help but let her mind drift into her past. "I've seen that look in Mom's eyes before," she whispered to Morgan, "and Wanda doesn't have a clue what Mrs. Eileen Chambers, 'special-needs therapist at large,' has in store for her. I really wanted to tell that kid to shape up, but I don't think she's ready to listen."

"I'm afraid she's going to have to learn the hard way," Morgan whispered back.

"Wanda's going to wish she *were* shoveling a ton of horse manure in about one minute."

"She just might get her wish," Skye said as she went into her bedroom. "She'll find out soon enough not to mess with Mom."

After a gourmet lasagna meal complete with salad, garlic bread, and brownies, the girls, including a grumpy Wanda, helped clean up. Mr. Chambers then headed downstairs to his computer repair shop while Mrs. Chambers went into the living room to read the paper. The three girls and two dogs followed her into the room. When Mrs. Chambers sat on the sofa the dogs jumped up and joined her, one on each side.

Wanda eyed the dogs with suspicion. "Can I shoot pool now?" she asked Mrs. Chambers.

"You tell me," Mrs. Chambers. "What had I asked you to do first?"

"Do my homework and show these two yo-yos my bedroom." Wanda parked her hands on her hips.

"Where's the English paper?"

"It's not done yet," Wanda informed her.

"And you're supposed to show *whom* your bedroom?" Mrs. Chambers grabbed the newspaper and opened it. She peered over the top and stared at Wanda.

"Oh, all right," Wanda growled, folding her arms. "You want them to see my bedroom."

"And their names are?" Mrs. Chambers peaked her eyebrows.

"Skye and Morgan," Wanda mumbled.

"Excuse me?" Mrs. Chambers said.

"Skye and Morgan!" Wanda said louder and more distinctly.

"That's right," Mrs. Chambers said, shifting her glance to the paper. "After you give them an exclusive tour and show me that completed assignment, you may shoot pool for a half hour."

"A half hour?" Wanda moaned, placing her hands back on her hips. "Is that all?"

Skye and Morgan waited in silence.

Mrs. Chambers never looked up from her paper. "Wanda, we went over all of this the first day you arrived. You have to earn your privileges at Keystone Stables, and you can start by working on your attitude. Consider yourself fortunate that you have—let me say *might have*—thirty minutes to yourself tonight."

Wanda turned and stormed back down the hallway. "C'mon, you two. It's showtime in my bedroom."

"I've heard your room is really cool," Skye said, leading the way with Morgan close behind. The two dogs followed, their toenails clicking on the hardwood floor.

At her doorway, Wanda turned and pointed at the dogs. "Keep those fleabags out. If they put one of their grimy paws in here, they're dead meat."

Skye and Morgan both looked at the Westies. "Sorry, fellas," Skye said. "Go find Mom."

As the dogs turned and raced back to Mrs. Chambers, Skye and Morgan entered Wanda's room. Wanda had already stretched out on her bed, hands behind her head and high-top black sneakers planted into the spread. Morgan parked herself in the doorway.

Skye examined every corner of the bedroom with its new décor. The curtains, bedspread, and throw rug had billiard paraphernalia designs set in a dark green background. On one wall hung three posters of professional pool players, all men, posing at fancy billiard tables.

On the wall between two windows hung a green clock that had a tiny billiard ball for each number and mini pool sticks for the hands. Wanda's dresser hosted two trophies, each about six inches high, nestled in the middle of a messy pile of junk.

"Wow, these decorations are really nice," Skye said sincerely. "But where'd you find all this pool stuff?"

Wanda answered Skye almost with a tone of decency. "I'm sure you have no idea that in the back of the Super Sports Emporium in the mall is a whole section with pool stuff. They had all of it there. I'm also sure you have no idea that there's a pool room with four brand-new pool tables behind the mall. The woman said she'd take me there sometime to shoot a few games."

"Nope," Skye said. "I didn't know that. And who's *the woman?*"

"My prison warden, Eileen Chambers," Wanda grumbled.

"I hope she never catches you calling her that," Skye said. "Mom's one tough cookie, Wanda. You better not mess with her. And Dad's no pushover either."

"She won't," Wanda sassed. "And I can take both of them on with one hand tied behind my back."

"You'll be sorry," Skye warned.

"I didn't even know they made pool stuff like this. It is definitely unique," Morgan said, gazing around the room. "Well, I've got to get back to my algebra or I'll pay for it big time tomorrow." She backed out the doorway and wheeled down the hallway.

Okay, Skye planned. *Let's see if we can break the ice with this kid.* "What are those two trophies?" she asked.

"I won them in Harrisburg at two different junior billiard competitions last year," Wanda boasted. "There were about a dozen boys and only two other girls beside me."

Skye strolled over to the dresser and picked up one of the trophies. "They are really—"

31

Slam!

Skye felt herself spun around and pinned tightly against the wall while the trophy went flying out of her hand. Wanda shoved her nose right against Skye's, and Skye stared into two brown eyes that flamed with hatred.

"Now listen, horse breath!" Wanda barked. "Get this straight. Keep your hands off my stuff. It's your stinking fault I'm in this stinking mess. I don't like you, and I don't like this dump. As soon as I can make some connections, I'm outta here! So just stay out of my way. Got it?" Wanda released her grip but still stood only inches away from Skye, staring her down and almost breathing fire.

Wanda, this is the second time you've caught me off guard, Skye stewed as she tightened her fists. *One sharp jab to your smart-aleck belly, and you'll be doubled over in pain. Jesus, what should I do?*

"Wanda," Skye said with a sincere smile. "I'm praying for you. You'd really like it here if you'd give us a chance to help you."

Pow!

Wanda seemed to reel as if Skye had planted a set of brass knuckles into her stomach. She quickly took a step back, and, with a look of confusion draped all over her face, she stood like her sneakers were nailed to the floor.

"What's going on back here?" Mrs. Chambers said, poking her head in the doorway.

Wanda quickly scooped up the trophy and retreated to her former position on the bed while Skye leaned on the side of the dresser.

"Nothing," Wanda said. "We're just looking at some of my stuff."

"Skye?" Mrs. Chambers said with her all-knowing tone.

"It's okay, Mom." Skye's glance darted from her mom to Wanda and back to her mom again. "We're cool."

Wanda's glance met Skye's with another brand-new look, one of apprehension. She looked like she was expecting Skye to tell every dirty little detail of the last few seconds.

"I heard a loud bang," Mrs. Chambers said. "It sounded like the roof fell in."

Skye saw Wanda open her mouth, ready to say something. "I dropped Wanda's trophy," Skye said and then gave Wanda another heartfelt smile. "Everything's okay. Really."

Wanda stared back at Skye, and just for a split second, Skye thought she saw something completely different on Wanda's face, something she had never seen before. The hint of a genuine smile.

Thank you, Lord, Skye prayed, giving Wanda another smile. *I think you and I got the upper hand in this round.*

chapter four

S kye reached forward and stroked Champ's neck. "Mom, is Dad bringing another horse home today?"

"Well, honey," Mrs. Chambers said, "it's not often that he gets a free Saturday to go to a horse auction. I know he's had his eye on a Mustang, and he learned that there was one for sale today. Don't be a bit surprised if he and the girls pull in here later today with one in the trailer."

Behind the large fenced-in Keystone Stables pasture, Skye and Mrs. Chambers trotted their mounts on a muddy road that trailed through the woods to Piney Hollow, the wilderness campsite and outdoor chapel that Skye loved so much. Skye rode Champ next to Mrs. Chambers on her dun mare, Lucy. Tippy and Tyler were having the time of their lives, romping and sniffing every tree within their noses' reach. Although a brisk wind tousled the horses' manes and tails, a cloudless sun coaxed Skye to unzip her coat and take off her gloves. There was nothing in the whole wide world that Skye enjoyed more than riding Champ and being with Mrs. Chambers to talk about "things."

The first day of spring had already tickled nature, and although it was not yet April, Skye drank in the signs of new life emerging in every direction. Shade trees glistened with bright green buds that were squeezing their way out of drab brown limbs that had been dormant all winter long. The earth, thawing from its chill, smelled "new," and birds chirped with a trill of delight. Skye spotted a few stray daffodils and crocuses hugging the fence posts along the back pasture, and the honking of geese high overhead heralded the news that warmer days were just around the corner.

"Do you really think he'll come home with a wild Mustang?" Skye asked.

The wind teased Mrs. Chambers' Stetson, forcing her to tighten her chin string. "If he finds the right one," she said. "He's wanted to have one from out West for years. If the price is right, we'll have horse number six. Since you and Chad took that course at the horse whispering camp last summer, we figured you two can help train the new member of our equine family."

"Chad and me?" Skye said while her heart took a funny beat. "I'd love to try. I'm sure he would too."

"I'm so glad you had the opportunity to learn that technique," Mrs. Chambers said. "With horse whispering so popular all around the world, I look for the days of *breaking* horses to soon be a thing of the past."

Skye nodded as her mind drifted. "Mom, when Sam Kline, the director of the horse whispering camp, showed us old pictures of how cowboys whipped and spurred horses and used twitches on their noses and did other horrible stuff to make them listen, I cried like a baby. Horses used to obey out of fear or pain. Now with the horse whispering techniques, they bond with their trainers and actually enjoy learning. It is so cool."

Ten minutes of conversation later, Skye and Mrs. Chambers rode out of the woods to the small clearing at the base of three sloping hills. In the center of Piney Hollow under a cluster of pines rested the chuck wagon, still wrapped up in its winter clothing of canvas tarps and rope tie-downs. Skye glanced to the left to the outdoor chapel with its stone cross and few rows of hewn tree-trunk benches. A gust of wind blew sharply, and a small whirl of leaves danced across the benches. No one but Mrs. Chambers knew how very special that chapel was to Skye.

The horses walked next to the wagon to a wooden hitching post where Mrs. Chambers and Skye dismounted, wound the reins around the railing, and walked to the chapel. Skye took off her hardhat and ran her fingers through her long hair as it whisked in another sharp gust. Tippy and Tyler went running off into another sniffing adventure.

Mrs. Chambers sat on the bench in front of the cross and gestured for Skye to sit beside her. "Skye, what runs through your mind when you come here?"

Skye sat down and stared at the cross. "I think of how stupid I was, and how you loved me—how God loved me—no matter how many dumb things I did. When I think of that stunt I pulled, trying to jump Champ over the wall, and how Dad tumbled off his horse—"

"Skye, we don't need to rehearse all the mistakes you've made. Lord knows, I've made my own share as well. God did a wonderful work in your life, and he can change Wanda, too, can't he?"

"Oh, so you want to talk to me about Wanda," Skye said, staring into Mrs. Chambers' deep blue eyes.

"Yes, honey," Mrs. Chambers answered with a warm smile. "I know that it's going to be rough for a while with Wanda. I also know that she could be dangerous, so please be very careful around her. Tom and I are watching her every move, but she's street smart. She thinks she knows how to hoodwink the whole bunch of us. I just want you and Morgan to be on your guard." She wrapped her arm around Skye's shoulders and drew her close.

"Thanks, Mom," Skye said.

As Mrs. Chambers released her grip, Skye stood and looked back at Champ. "I remember how I hated everything when I first came here, even him. Wanda reminds me an awful lot of myself. I want to help her, Mom, but she told me to stay out of her way."

"I figured she did. She doesn't want anyone in her space." Mrs. Chambers stood, and she and Skye headed toward the horses. "All good things take time, honey. God has a perfect plan for Wanda's life, with perfect timing. We need to try to help her see the truth and then stay out of *his* way as he works and changes her from the inside out."

"She's awful mad about something," Skye said. "Where are her parents?"

"Her father's in prison and her mother died a few years ago."

"How'd her mom die?"

"I'm not quite sure. I think Wanda's grandmother mentioned something about her having a bad heart."

"Well, at least she knows where they are."

"Skye, maybe someday God will open the door for you to find out what happened to your parents. I know that troubles you."

"Maybe someday," Skye said. "In the meantime, I guess we just have to concentrate on Wanda. I'll have to pray harder for her."

Mrs. Chambers touched Skye's arm. "That's a great idea, Skye. Let's take time right now," she said, and they bowed their heads.

"Lord," Mrs. Chambers began, "we ask that you help us with Wanda. We know that she's hard to love, but we know that you love her as much as you love us. Please help her to realize that we want to help her. And, Lord, we pray for her to accept you into her life."

"And, dear God," Skye said, "help Morgan and me to know what to do and when. We want to be patient with Wanda, so I'm asking for patience. Please."

"In Jesus' name, amen," Mrs. Chambers added.

"Amen," Skye said.

Back at the barn, just as Skye and Mrs. Chambers turned their mounts out to pasture, Mr. Chambers, Morgan and Wanda pulled in with the two-horse trailer, occupied by one wild Mustang.

As the truck and its rig stopped in front of the barn, Wanda jumped out of the passenger side of the truck. "That horse is nuts!" she said. "And he's nuts for buying it." She pointed at Mr. Chambers who was getting out of the driver's side of the cab.

"What do you have back there, Tom?" Mrs. Chambers asked as she retrieved Morgan's wheelchair from the cab.

"I bought a six-year-old tobiano pinto gelding," Mr. Chambers said. "I finally got my Mustang from out West."

Wanda leaned against the fender of the truck. "That horse is a wild maniac!" she said, folding her arms. "He kicked and bucked the whole time they loaded him on the trailer."

Skye walked behind the truck and watched as Mr. Chambers carefully approached the back of the trailer and unhooked the latch that held the ramp in place. Carefully, an inch at a time, he let down the ramp, staying clear of the horse's back legs. Without cause, the horse lifted one rear leg and let out a swift kick, just missing Mr. Chambers' arm.

"A black-and-white pinto!" Skye said. "Wow, he is nasty, Dad, but he's also beautiful."

"Beautiful, yes," Mr. Chambers said. "But wild as a March hare too." He backed away from the trailer, lifted his Stetson and, despite the chilly air, wiped a layer of sweat from his forehead onto his coat sleeve. "He's a rescued animal. The last joker who owned him whipped him and half starved him. Thankfully, the PA Animal Rescue Squad got the horse before more damage was done. They've been able to put some weight on him, but we're going to have our hands full training him."

Morgan turned her wheelchair to face the trailer. "His name is Rebel. How appropriate is that?" Her glance darted Wanda's way.

"I want all of you girls to move way back." Mr. Chambers pointed toward the back porch of the house behind Skye. "In fact, that's as good a place as any to watch the action. Eileen, please be ready to open the corral gate."

Skye and Morgan immediately headed toward the porch.

"You too, Wanda," Skye heard Mr. Chambers say. "Now."

"Tsk," Wanda said as she slid her hands into her jean pockets and sauntered toward the back porch.

Skye chewed her lip as she watched Mr. Chambers cautiously walk into the right side of the trailer and reach over the partition to his left to loosen the lead rope that held Rebel's head steady during transport.

"Easy, Rebel," Mr. Chambers said. Then he clicked his tongue and slowly started to ease the horse out of the trailer. Mrs. Chambers headed toward the training corral just a few yards away where she quickly unlatched the gate, swung it open, and stepped out of the way.

"Easy, fella." Mr. Chambers had the lead rope wound tightly around both hands as Rebel inched his way back and off the ramp.

As the Mustang backed out of the trailer, Skye studied every muscle in his powerful body. Eyes wild with fright, the horse took a few more steps back while Mr. Chambers quickly walked down the ramp. For a moment, Rebel and

Mr. Chambers stood in place with only the horse's long, flowing, black-and-white mane and tail whisking in the breeze. The horse arched his neck, swiveled his ears and then let out a nervous snort as he explored the strange place he was about to call his home.

An inch at a time, Mr. Chambers crept his hand toward the horse, aiming to slip his fingers around the halter. "Easy, boy," he said, "no one's going to hurt you."

"No one will hurt you, boy," Skye repeated her dad's words, but no one was listening.

Just as Mr. Chambers touched the halter, the horse yanked up his head, let out a piercing whinny, and reared up on his hind legs. Like pedals on a bike, the horse's front legs pawed at the air within inches of Mr. Chambers' head. All the while, the horse screamed high-pitched whinnies as though someone were beating him with a whip.

Skye leaned forward on the porch railing and her heart raced with fear. "Dad, watch out!" she yelled. "He's going to kill you!"

chapter five

M r. Chambers stumbled backward, losing his footing. He tumbled onto the trailer ramp and sent his Stetson flying. Spooked by the hat, Rebel reared up again and yanked the lead rope from Mr. Chambers' hands.

Suddenly from behind the trailer, a lasso loop sailed through the air and slipped over Rebel's flailing head.

"Way to go, Mom!" Skye yelled.

"She has him!" Morgan yelled.

Skye stretched forward, watching Mrs. Chambers who had just thrown the lasso and was tying her end of the rope around one of the corral fence posts. Rebel yanked and pulled, reared and neighed, but Mrs. Chambers' tie held secure.

"I've got him, Tom!" Mrs. Chambers yelled.

"This is like some kind of Wild West show with Rebel the Wonder Horse showing off big time," Skye said.

"I hope no one gets hurt," Morgan said.

"That horse is nuts." Wanda's brain was stuck with only one thought.

Mr. Chambers scrambled to his feet and groped at the lead rope that dangled and bounced from Rebel's head. Finally, he was able to grab it and pull it in the opposite direction of Mrs. Chamber's tether. Now he had Rebel where he wanted him — between a crosstie and unable to do much of anything but kick.

"They got him!" Skye said.

"I'm telling you, that horse is nuts."

"Wanda, you're getting your point across, loud and clear," Skye grumbled.

"He won't be nutso for long," Morgan said. "Keystone Stables is a place to get un-nutsoed whether you're a horse ... or a kid."

"Eileen," Mr. Chambers yelled, "keep the rope taut while I coax him into the corral!"

While Mrs. Chambers pulled, Mr. Chambers slowly eased off his rope, forcing the horse to take the lead toward the corral. Rebel snorted, pranced, and yanked, but trapped in the crosstie, that was all he could do to show his extreme displeasure with the entire situation.

When Rebel barreled into the corral, Mr. Chambers dropped his end of the rope and slammed the gate shut. He then grabbed Mrs. Chambers' lasso and cajoled the horse toward him with Rebel on the inside of the corral and Mr. and Mrs. Chambers on the outside.

In a lather of sweat, Rebel realized the uselessness of his fury and started to settle down. He planted all four hooves firmly on the ground and stood still as a statue in a Civil War museum. Then one cautious step at a time, with a series of snorts and head bobs and his mane and tail whisking freely, he inspected the two annoying humans.

Mr. Chambers climbed onto the bottom rail of the corral fence, and as Rebel stepped within arm's reach, Mr. Chambers carefully unclipped the horse's lead rope. With the lasso, he drew the horse within inches of the tie post and double-knotted the rope. He then backed off the fence, scooped up his hat, and, drenched in perspiration, he and Mrs. Chambers joined the girls on the porch.

"We'll just let him calm down for an hour or so before I try to get him into the barn," Mr. Chambers said.

"Dad," Skye said, "is he damaged beyond repair?"

"Well," Mr. Chambers said, "I've always wanted a *wild* Mustang from the West, and I think I got my wish this time. I bought him because I think he's trainable. There's always hope. He just needs some TLC, but it's going to take some time. We'll get that puppy in shape sooner or later."

Wanda sneered, "Puppy? Yeah, right. He's more like a raging werewolf."

Mr. Chambers looked directly into Wanda's eyes. "When animals are hurt as badly as this one, it takes them just as long to get over the pain as it does kids that are hurt."

"But there's always hope." Mrs. Chambers also gave Wanda her undivided attention. "Especially when we have God's help."

Wanda folded her arms and looked away.

Hmm, Skye observed. *She doesn't have much to say now.* "When can Chad and I start working with Rebel?" she asked as she shifted her attention to the horse.

Mr. Chambers smoothed his mustache and then rubbed his chin. "Let's plan for a couple of weeks from now. While you're at school, I'll start the horse whispering process and get the kick out of him. From that point on, you and Chad can continue."

"Yeah." Morgan giggled. "Rebel doesn't know what's coming. In no time at all, he'll change from an I-don't-wanna-do-nothing Mustang grouch to an I-wanna-be-your-equine-friend happy trail horse."

"No way," Wanda jeered. "This I gotta see."

Mrs. Chambers gave Skye and Morgan a radiant smile. "Greater miracles than that have happened at Keystone Stables. Haven't they, girls?"

"Yup," Skye said.

"You've said it, Mrs. C.," Morgan added.

Mr. Chambers slipped his arm around his wife's shoulders. "Well, dear, what's cooking in the kettle for supper? I'm so hungry I could eat a horse—ah, but not that one." He pointed toward Rebel.

"Steak and baked potatoes on the grill," Mrs. Chambers said. "Minus the horse."

"We could have horseradish," Skye suggested with a giggle.

"Okay, enough horsing around," Mr. Chambers said. "Let's mosey on in to the feed stall."

While everyone joined in a hearty laugh, Skye noticed that Wanda didn't move a muscle.

"I'm going to mend a fence down in the pasture," Mr. Chambers said to Skye and Chad as he hopped in his truck and started to pull away from the training corral. "I'll be within earshot if you need me."

"Okay, Mr. C.," Chad said. "Thanks."

On a beautiful April afternoon two Saturdays after Rebel arrived, Skye and Chad managed to get him into the training corral where they were about to begin their horse whispering techniques. Although Mr. Chambers had, indeed, gotten the kick out of him and had begun working him on a longe line, Rebel still balked and pranced the opposite direction when any human got too close. He made it perfectly clear that as far as allowing anyone to touch him or tack him, his answer was a clear-as-crystal "no way."

"Easy, boy," Skye said, closing the gate behind her. She cautiously detached the lead rope from the horse's halter and coiled the rope in her hands. Chad stood along the sidelines ready to offer assistance when needed. He squared his black Stetson and spoke softly. "Skye, remember what Sam said at the horse whispering camp. An abused horse takes longer to bond with us than a wild one fresh off the plains. Just take your time."

"Gotcha," she said. As she carefully reached to touch Rebel's muzzle, the animal reared and whinnied, his eyes wild with fear.

Skye stepped back, allowing the horse to relax. He pawed the ground, snorted, and backed up. Pivoting his powerful body, he faced his long flowing tail toward Skye. In stark defiance, he once again stood perfectly still and focused on the barn. With ears pricked forward and neck arched out over the fence, his sleek black-and-white coat sparkled in the warm spring sun.

"He is one gorgeous hunk of horse flesh, isn't he, Skye?" Chad said.

"He sure is, and I can't wait to ride him. And I'm going to, sooner or later." Skye took one end of her lead rope and started twirling it. Advancing toward Rebel, she spoke loudly to get his attention. "Hey, Rebel, boy. Let's do some longeing without the rope. What do you say, fella?"

Starting the process to bond with the horse, Skye used an advance-and-retreat method that she had practiced at camp. Gently, she worked Rebel by pitching one end of her long lead rope at his hindquarters while talking to him, thus forcing him to retreat or circle the perimeter of the corral. In the center of the corral, Skye's eyes and body followed every move the trotting horse made.

Skye planned that when Rebel tired of running and stopped, she would try to advance, staring eyeball to eyeball with the horse, and reach to touch his face. If he would allow her to make contact, she then would retreat and wait for him to come to her. At that point, Rebel would recognize her as the leader of his herd. She and the horse would bond, and he'd trust her enough to allow her to touch him all over his body, further his training, and make him a reliable mount. But Skye knew this horse had been damaged—badly—and it might take weeks before she would see anything happen at all.

For several minutes, Skye forced Rebel to retreat. When she withdrew the rope and he stopped, she made him advance. Just as her hand touched the horse's nose, a truck passing in front of Keystone Stables backfired, sending Rebel into a frenzy. He jerked up his head, let out a screeching whinny, and pivoted toward the fence, turning his tail toward Skye. With another loud nicker, he arched his neck and dug his hooves firmly into the ground. While he snorted, his ears swiveled like some kind of equine radar machine.

"Hey, Chad, old buddy!" Skye heard a familiar, and unwelcomed, voice yelling from the backyard. She slipped out of the corral and joined Chad at the same time Wanda arrived in her boys' clothes, baseball cap and all.

"Hi, Wanda," Skye said.

"What's happening?" Chad said, tipping his Stetson toward the girl.

Wanda punched Chad in the arm and threw a quick glance at Rebel. "Looks like nothing much is happening with Dog Meat there. What a trip."

"Wanda, all good things take time," Skye said. "I think we would have made progress if that truck hadn't backfired."

"Yeah, yeah, yeah," Wanda slurred and in the next breath said, "Hey, Chad, how about a game of Nine Ball? The woman said I could take a half hour break from my science project while she ran to the grocery store." Wanda pointed her thumb toward the house, then swirled her index finger. "Whoopdeedoo. A measly half hour."

"It's better than nothing," Skye said.

Wanda completely ignored Skye. "What'd ya say, Chad?"

"Maybe later," Chad said, reaching for the rope in Skye's hands. "I want to try my hand with Rebel."

"Can I watch?" Wanda asked Chad.

"As long as you stay back here and don't make any noise," he said. "His kind don't like distractions."

"I want to watch *you*, not him," Wanda said, smirking at Skye.

Skye felt her face turn red hot, hotter than it had been in ages. Bubbling like a volcano ready to explode, anger that she thought she had long learned to control turned her stomach upside down. She stared at Wanda, gave her a return smirk, and turned toward the house. "I'm going for some lemonade. Anyone else want some?"

"Sure," Chad said.

"Got any beer?" Wanda cackled.

"You'll find that three miles down the road," Skye said.

"I'll pass," Wanda said. "Watching Chad is all I want right now."

Ignoring Wanda, Chad crawled into the training coral and focused on Rebel.

Tears flooding her eyes, Skye rushed into the house, ran into her bedroom, slammed the door, and crashed onto her bed.

"I don't like her. God, I know it's wrong, but I just don't like her," she said, and soaked her bedspread with tears.

47

Scratched again!" Skye said after her cue ball dropped in a side pocket of the pool table.

"I'll never be as good as Chad—or *her*—at this game," Skye lamented.

Morgan sat at a computer playing her favorite online game, "Battleship," with someone from Spain. "This is too cool," she said. "This kid's in tenth grade too, and he's learning English. His name is Francisco." Morgan paused and then said, "What was that, Skye? You'll never get as good as who?"

"Wanda." Skye mounted her cue stick in a wall rack and sat next to Morgan. "It's useless."

"Skye, she's been playing for years," Morgan said. "So what's the big deal anyway? You can run circles around her when it comes to horses, or homework, or just being a decent human being. All she's got going for her is a good game of pool."

"Chad can shoot real good too," Skye said.

Morgan relaxed into her wheelchair and turned toward Skye. "Ah ha, I knew it. You're worried about her moving in on him, aren't you?"

Without an answer, Skye looked at her monitor and turned on her computer.

Morgan tapped Skye on the shoulder. "Hey," she said.

Skye looked at her foster sister and figured it was time for a sisterly chat. *Morgan's so good at these things*, she thought. "Oh, all right. Yes, I am worried."

"Thought so." Morgan nodded and her freckled face lit up with an understanding smile. "Skye, you know exactly what Mrs. C. would say if you were having this conversation with her, don't you?"

"Yes-s-s." Skye ran her fingers through her hair and turned back to the computer. She loaded a dirt bike racing game and worked the controls.

"You're way too young to date, and so is Chad. He's not your territory. And besides, God has your future—and your love life—all planned out."

"I know," Skye said. "It's really stupid to feel this way, and I think I need God to help me with this mess. But Chad and I are such good friends. I don't want anything, or anyone, to spoil it."

"Nothing's going to spoil it." Morgan said. "And you don't need to worry about Wanda. I'm sure Chad's not interested in her—she's not his type. Give me a break."

"I know that he wants a nice Christian girl," Skye said. "He told me that once."

"Well, need I say more?"

"When I look at Wanda, I can't believe that I was like that once."

"I don't think I was that bad," Morgan said, "but it's only because of God that I'm where I am today."

"Did you know Wanda smokes?" Skye asked. "One day last week I saw her throwing a cigarette butt in the yard when she came out of the barn. She'd better be careful around all that hay."

"Yeah, I can smell smoke on her. Yesterday I went into the bathroom right after she came out, and it smelled like a tobacco factory in there."

"Do you think Mom and Dad know she's smoking?"

"What do you think?"

Skye rolled her eyes. "Nothing gets past them."

"I'm sure Mrs. C. is counseling Wanda about all this stuff. But nothing's going to change overnight."

"Speaking of overnight," Skye said, "I thought I heard some strange noises a few nights since Wanda moved in. Do you think she prowls around when we're all asleep? I bet she's using the phone to call her gang in Harrisburg."

"With her room at the other end of the hall, I haven't heard much," Morgan said. "But I heard Mrs. C. talking to her one day about Wanda not sleeping in her own bedroom."

"What? Where's she sleeping?"

"Believe it or not, either in the hayloft in the barn or here on the pool table."

"You've got to be kidding. Who wouldn't want to sleep in a nice soft bed? That is weird."

"I have a feeling that Wanda's had it pretty rough. Who knows? Maybe she doesn't even have a bed at home. Remember, she's been running with a gang for years. She's probably used to sleeping on the floor more than on a bed. And I heard Mrs. C. talking to Wanda about some bad dreams Wanda was having. So there must be something going on there that we don't know about."

"When you think about that, it's really sad. She'd almost be pretty if she'd clean up her act. I've never seen such long curly eyelashes before. I wonder if anything or anyone will ever convince her to change."

"God can," Morgan said. "But we've got to be willing to do our part. We need to just try to help her. She needs Jesus in her life before anything else starts to change."

"Even though I don't like her, I'd really like to help her, if she'd just listen to some advice. We've been where she is. But for now, I guess the best thing we can do is stay out of her way."

"Sooner or later, Skye, she'll realize that she needs a friend—a real friend. That's when we need to be ready to be one."

"I'd like to be there for her when that day comes," Skye said. "I really would."

"Me, too," Morgan said, backing her wheelchair away from the computer and glancing at her watch. "Well, I think it's time to get supper ready. Mrs. C. should be here any minute."

Skye glanced at her watch. "Wow, I didn't realize it was so late. If you want to toss the salad, I'll stir-fry the chicken. We'll have the stuff ready in the shake of a horse's tail."

"Not Rebel's." Morgan laughed. "He's too stubborn."

"Girls," Mr. Chambers said as he wiped his mustache with a napkin, "this supper is terrific. You're getting better in the kitchen every day."

The three girls sat with Mr. and Mrs. Chambers at the dining room table enjoying teenage gourmet cooking. Tippy and Tyler found their usual place on the floor, one on each side of Mrs. Chambers' chair. The topics of conversation varied as much as the colors of the rainbow. Everyone joined in except Wanda, who barely ate anything and played with her food. Her answers were curt when anyone directed a question her way. With her bedraggled hair making its own statement, she crouched in her chair and didn't crack a smile.

"I almost burned the chicken, Dad," Skye said. "It's a good thing Morgan was there to keep me focused."

"Were you staring out the window at the horses?" Mrs. Chambers asked. "I know where your heart is."

"Guilty, your honoress." Skye giggled. "Morgan's the cook, I'm the equestrian, and Wanda's the pool shark."

"Even pool sharks have to eat," Mr. Chambers said. Everyone laughed but Wanda.

Mr. Chambers took one last bite of his tossed salad. "Now don't forget, girls, that next week we have special meetings at church from Monday to Wednesday. Our missions conference starts on Sunday."

When the subject of church and God came up, Wanda slid down further into her chair.

"Oh, I did forget," Skye said.

"Me too," said Morgan. "I can't wait to see the slides of South Africa."

Without looking up, Wanda spouted out, "What—is a missions conference?"

Mrs. Chambers took a sip of water. "Wanda."

I know she's waiting for Wanda to look at her, Skye thought.

Silence.

Finally, Wanda looked at Mrs. Chambers.

"It's a series of meetings we have in our church every year that keeps us, the members of the church, informed about the work our missionaries are doing all around the world. Missionaries are really like pastors, but they serve mostly in other countries."

Wanda scrunched up her face and folded her arms. "How exciting," she sneered. "I think I'll pass."

"Sorry, Wanda," Mr. Chambers said. "We'll all be there, every night. You might be surprised at what you learn about how people live in other parts of the world. God's been so good to us here in this country. So many folks in other places have almost nothing."

"I ain't never had it so good," Wanda said. "When Pop got sent up and Mom died, I had to live with Gram. She's always been sick. That's how good that God of yours has been to me."

"Wanda," Mrs. Chambers said, "God is just waiting to bless your life, but you're fighting him."

"I don't need no God that would let my mother die."

"At least you know where your parents are," Skye said with kind intent. "I don't have a clue where mine are."

Wanda gave Skye another strange look, almost as if she was genuinely interested in what Skye was saying.

Maybe she's starting to listen, Skye thought. *Just maybe.*

"Wanda, we'd like to discuss something that affects the whole family," Mrs. Chambers said.

Wanda took her good old time looking at Mrs. Chambers. "What?" she snapped.

"Mr. Chambers and I feel it's not safe for you to be sleeping in the barn, especially with your smoking habit."

The expression on Wanda's face turned to pure shock. Skye placed a safe bet that Wanda was thinking, *How'd they know?*

Mr. Chambers added, "And, yes, we've known from the beginning that you've been sneaking to the barn or down to the game room to sleep, then sneaking back to your bedroom right before we all get up."

While Skye worked at her food, her glance darted around the table like she was watching a ping-pong game. Morgan did the same.

"Wanda, dear, there's no need for you to be sneaking around," Mrs. Chambers said. "If you're uncomfortable sleeping in your bedroom, we can accommodate you, at least for a little while."

"That's right," Mr. Chambers said, and then he sipped his drink. "We have a futon stored in my shop downstairs. We'll move that into the game room if you'd like. There's a place for it in the corner next to the computers."

"All we ask is that you keep that corner neat and you don't try to sleep when we have the Youth for Truth kids here on game night," Mrs. Chambers said.

Everyone burst into laughter except Wanda, but this time Skye detected the slightest hint of a smile on Wanda's face.

"So," Mr. Chambers said, "Can we have your word of honor that you'll not sneak to the barn anymore?"

Wanda said nothing and stared at her plate still half-full of food.

Mrs. Chambers finished her drink. "Wanda, our family, the one you are part of for the next year, discusses everything. Our love for one another is built on trust. If you don't like something, tell us about it. We want to help you and we want you to feel like part of this family." Mrs. Chambers reached and touched Wanda's hand. "We love you."

Although Wanda abruptly pulled away without a word, she stared into Mrs. Chambers' eyes as if she were thinking, *Is she for real?*

"Yes, she's for real," Skye said.

"And about the cigarettes," Mr. Chambers said. "We'd appreciate your turning all of them into us like you were supposed to when you first came. With God's help, and ours, you can kick that habit before it takes a good hold of your system."

"And now is as good a time as any." Mrs. Chambers smiled at Wanda. "Come on. I'll escort you to your room and we can have ourselves a little hunt."

"Tsk," Wanda said. She pushed away from the table and trudged back down the hallway like a prisoner on her way to the gallows.

When Wanda was out of earshot, Morgan whispered, "Mr. C., she's not going to give them up that easily."

Skye added, "When Mom's not watching her at Maranatha, she can get a fresh supply from the other kids."

"We know," Mr. Chambers said. "We know."

chapter seven

"Easy, Rebel!" Chad said, trying to calm down the wild Mustang in the training corral the next Saturday. As usual, when either Chad or Skye worked the horse, Rebel would allow them to get only within inches of his muzzle, and then he'd balk.

Skye stood outside the corral, watching the progress, or lack of it. "He's one stubborn mule, isn't he, Chad?"

"You can say that again." Chad slipped out of the corral between the rails and joined Skye, who had crossed her arms on the top rail of the fence.

"He must have been abused awfully bad," Skye said. "But he'll come around. I just know it."

"Patience and tough love, my dear." Chad gave Skye his best dimpled smile.

Skye gulped and her heart did back flips. *He called me "dear."* She gave Chad a return smile and then glanced at her watch. "It's two o'clock already. We've been out here over an hour, and nothing's happened yet. It's been two weeks since we started."

"Speaking of nothing happening," Chad said, "how's Wanda, the other rebel, doing?"

"Why do you ask?" Skye said. *Yes, why would you ask about her, Chad Dressler!*

"Just curious," Chad said. "A few of us Youth for Truth kids are praying for her."

Skye leaned her chin on her arm and stared at Rebel, who was, as usual, facing in the opposite direction. "Not much better, I guess. She won't talk to me unless it's a slam. Her favorite name for me is 'horse breath.' Sheesh! She hangs out at the pool table all the time, and she even sleeps in the game room. If Mom would let Wanda eat there, she'd never come out. Really strange."

"I saw that futon next to the computers and wondered about it," Chad said.

"That futon is right underneath my bedroom, and you should hear the way she yells in her sleep. She has really bad nightmares, and that's probably why she won't sleep in her bedroom. It's right next to Mom's and Dad's room, and she doesn't want them to hear her carrying on."

"Who knows what might have happened to her when she was a little kid," Chad said. "Do you know why her father's in prison?"

"Nope. She won't talk about it. At least, not with me. She won't talk about anything with me."

"How's she doing with her smoking?"

"I'm not sure. I haven't smelled any smoke on her lately, and I haven't seen any butts lying around anywhere, but she's street smart. She could be stashing them anywhere."

"Patience and tough love, my dear."

Dear? Twice in one day. Chad's smile sent Skye's heart into another aerobic routine.

"How's Rebel doing?" Mrs. Chambers asked, coming up behind Skye and Chad.

"No breakthrough yet, Mom." Skye turned toward Mrs. Chambers and saw Wanda standing right beside her.

"Hi, Wanda," Skye said.

As usual, Wanda donned her ball cap and same old clothes. But instead of her high top sneakers, Wanda was wearing riding boots.

Wanda barely glanced at Skye and said nothing.

Chad squared his Stetson. "Mrs. C., Sooner or later, Rebel's got to realize that we want to help him, not hurt him," he said and then added, "Howdy, Wanda."

"So, Wanda," Skye said staring at Wanda's boots, "I see your tootsies have a new wardrobe. That can only mean one thing: it's your big day to ride a horse."

"Whatever," Wanda grumbled, hanging her thumbs on her jean pockets and masquerading *tough*. "I rode horses lots when I was a kid."

Well, that's a barefaced lie, Skye thought. *She's just saying that to impress Chad.*

"So, you've ridden horses before, Wanda? How interesting," Chad said, giving Skye a quick wink.

Skye slipped out a sly smile then studied Wanda, noting an air of nervousness that oozed out all over, no matter how cool the girl tried to be. "I remember my first ride on Champ," Skye said, "and I was shaking in *my* boots until I realized how gorgeous and well-trained he was."

Mrs. Chambers beamed with obvious delight over Wanda's progress. "I think Wanda's ready to take that big step. She's already had a handful of lessons on grooming, tacking, and leading a horse. And she hasn't done half bad for someone who says she hates horses. Wanda, stay here, and I'll go get Lucy."

"You'll do great," Chad said to Wanda. "Just let the horse teach you. Lucy's got years of experience under her cinch, so it should be a cinch!"

Skye giggled, but Wanda folded her arms and just stared at Chad.

As Mrs. Chambers led Lucy out of the barn, Skye again studied Wanda's face, which almost seemed to light up at the sight of the horse. *I think she really does want to ride, but she's too stubborn to admit it.*

"Wanda and I are going into the pasture," Mrs. Chambers said to Skye and Chad. "You two may carry on your work with Rebel. I don't think we'll get in each other's way."

"Okay, Mom," Skye said as Chad slipped into the corral with Rebel. "We'll stay out of your horsehair, if you'll stay out of ours."

Everyone laughed but Wanda.

Skye woke up in the middle of the night with her mouth as dry as a ball of cotton. She rolled over and glanced at her clock's bold red numbers. "Two thirty," she moaned to herself. "I gotta have a drink."

Struggling to stay awake, she forced herself out of bed and slouched her way toward her bedroom door. As she glanced at the mirror, a bright light jabbed at her sleepy eyes. She rubbed them and looked again, then turned quickly toward the window. Her gaze drifted outside, down past the yard and to the barn, where billows of smoke and a geyser of orange flames were erupting out of the one corner of the hayloft.

"Oh, no!" she yelled. "The barn's on fire!" She charged out of her room to Mr. and Mrs. Chambers' door and pounded so hard the whole wall shook. "Mom, Dad! The barn's on fire! I'll call 911!"

"What?" Mrs. Chambers mumbled.

"The barn's on fire!" Skye screamed. "We've got to get the horses out!" She raced into the dining room and made the emergency call with her trembling hands barely able to hold the phone.

Mr. Chambers shot out of his room, still slipping into his shirt and buckling his belt. Mrs. Chambers followed right on his heels, yanking a sweatshirt over her disheveled hair. Both bore expressions of panic, the likes of which Skye had never seen before. Mr. Chambers charged out of the sliding glass door and sprinted toward the barn.

Grasping the door, Mrs. Chambers paused. "Skye, tell Morgan to stay in the house. Oh, and go down and get Wanda. She can help. Hurry."

Skye ran back the hall, banged on Morgan's door and burst into the room.

Morgan had already sat up and had turned on her light. "Skye!" A look of horror masked her face.

"Mom wants you to stay in the house," Skye ordered as she turned to leave. "Just pray."

Skye raced back into her room, tugged on her jeans and boots and scrambled toward the basement. She flipped on the light and hurried down the stairs two, three at a time. "Wanda!" she screamed, but Wanda was not there—and her bed was neatly made.

Skye tore out of the basement and ran as fast as her legs could go toward the barn.

Thick smoke billowed from the second floor where hay bales were stored, and flames licked boards around an open window. Mr. Chambers was desperately wielding water from a garden hose at the angry flames.

Hooves pounding the ground, Lucy bolted out of the barn. Ears plastered against her head and nostrils flaring, she ran past Skye, off into the cool dark of the night.

"Skye!" Mr. Chambers yelled. "Get the horses out!"

"Skye, in here!" Mrs. Chambers called. "Help me open these stalls and the horses will run out on their own!"

Skye darted into the barn filled with white smoke that was growing denser. Lungs burning with what she had already inhaled, she held her breath as long as she could, but her body soon demanded more air. Pressing her nose against her arm, she noticed that the lights were on. Through the swirling white film, Skye could see Mrs. Chambers moving quickly at the other end of the barn.

Skye ran toward Mrs. Chambers who was coughing and opening Rebel's stall. With a horse's natural fear of fire, Rebel needed no prodding. Releasing high-pitched squeals, he barreled out of the doorway, nearly trampling Skye on his way out.

In the distance, blaring sirens brought help closer and closer. Skye only prayed it wasn't too late.

Skye's lungs felt like she had breathed in the fire itself, and her eyes burned as she ran to Champ's stall, fumbled with the latch, and yanked open both Dutch doors. "Easy, Champ," she coughed as he nickered and pranced. She grabbed his halter and led him out of the stall toward the open doorway. "Go on, boy," she coughed, slapping him on his rump. "You're okay. Now go."

As though charging out of a starting gate at a racetrack, Champ took off.

Skye and Mrs. Chambers released the remaining four horses that raced out of the barn. Nose buried in her arm, Mrs. Chambers quickly surveyed the situation, and Skye did the same. Although smoke had penetrated the entire ground floor of the barn, Skye couldn't see any flames through her stinging, watery eyes.

"C'mon." Coughing, Mrs. Chambers started running toward the door. "We need to get some fresh air."

Skye followed Mrs. Chambers outside just as two screaming fire engines, a tanker, and an ambulance, all with flashing lights, barreled down the driveway and pulled a short distance from the barn. The trucks and their commotion lit up the place like a firemen's carnival. As far as Skye could tell, about ten firemen scrambled from the trucks and started their assigned tasks.

Moving to the far side of the barn, Mr. Chambers continued to spray water on the fire. "I think it just started!" he yelled to anyone who would listen.

"Is there anyone in the barn?" one fireman yelled.

"No!" Mr. Chambers yelled. "We just got all the horses out!"

Another fireman asked, "Do you have a pond on your property?"

"Yes," Mr. Chambers answered, "at the bottom of the fenced-in pasture."

"Freeburg's trucks should be here any sec," the fireman said. "Open your gate so their tanker can fill up."

Mr. Chambers dropped the hose and raced toward the gate.

Skye stared at the scene while two men quickly slid a large plastic holding tank off the truck and started pumping water from the tanker into it. One fireman grabbed some kind of line or hose from another truck and pulled it to the plastic tank where he plugged it in. Two other men shoulder-loaded a hose from the first truck and stretched it the length of the barn. A pair of men from another truck donned breathing apparatus, grabbed fire extinguishers and hatchets, and started toward the barn.

The men with the outstretched hose started spraying water on the flames in the loft while two men from the second truck prepped their hose.

Still coughing, Skye watched the firemen perform their duties with the precision that only drill after drill had produced. Every man knew exactly what to do to put out the fire and save the barn from total destruction.

Out of the ambulance hopped two EMTs. Carrying small cases, they rushed toward Mrs. Chambers and Skye. "Are you all right?" asked a chubby female in a navy blue uniform.

Mrs. Chambers gestured toward Skye and spoke through a series of coughs. "We... got our lungs full of smoke, but we're okay. Just let us... catch our breath."

"Do you need any oxygen?" a tall, thin EMT with a beard asked.

"I think... we're okay," Skye managed to say. "We were in the barn... just long enough to get the horses out."

Gasping, Mr. Chambers joined the group while his glare never left the barn.

"Sir," the male EMT asked Mr. Chambers, "are you okay?"

"Yeah, I'm fine," Mr. Chambers said. "I didn't breathe in any smoke... I'm just winded."

With blasting sirens and flashing lights, three more fire trucks and another ambulance barreled down the driveway. They clattered to the far side of the barn and pulled to a screeching halt. One busy fireman in front of the barn ran to the tanker and shouted something to the driver. As the firemen hopped off the engines, the tanker backed up, maneuvered around the other trucks, and headed toward the pond.

Mrs. Chambers grabbed Skye by both shoulders and glared into her face. "Skye ... where's Wanda?"

Skye's eyes grew as round as saucers. "Mom... I completely forgot to tell you... she wasn't in her bed." She then pointed at the barn. "She might be in there!"

"Wan-da!" Mrs. Chambers screamed and started running toward the barn, but Mr. Chambers grabbed her arm and stopped her. "You stay here!" he yelled. "I'll go in."

"You can't go in there!" an EMT yelled.

"I have to," he said. "One of our girls is in there!"

Mr. Chambers ran to a firemen gearing up and told him about Wanda.

"Mike!" the fireman yelled back to the hosemen. "There might be a kid in there. We're going in."

"Okay," one said. Turning his water on, he and his partner streamed a second powerful surge of water into the barn's loft.

Skye and Mrs. Chambers stood clearing their lungs and watching while Mr. Chambers followed the firemen into the barn. Skye glanced back at the house and saw

Morgan and two dogs looking out the sliding glass door. Flames from the fire and the flashing lights lit up the entire Keystone Stables yard. Skye took a quick count to make sure that all the horses were safe. All six had settled a comfortable distance from the fire and were indulging in an early morning snack of dewy grass.

Into the driveway pulled a pick-up truck that Skye knew belonged to their next-door neighbor, Mr. Garside. Just seconds behind, two other cars also pulled in. Mr. Garside jumped out of the truck and came running toward the group. The drivers of the other cars, also neighbors, came running.

"I heard the sirens!" Mr. Garside yelled with excitement. A John Deere ball cap fit snuggly on his gray head, and his plump, tanned face beaded with perspiration. "It looks like they got here in time."

"This is not a night to sleep soundly," another neighbor said, forcing out a laugh.

"Can we do anything to help?" the third man asked.

"One of our girls might be in there." Mrs. Chambers' voice quivered as she wiped a barrage of tears from her face and tried to clear her lungs. "She likes to sleep in the barn."

"I'm going in," Mr. Garside said, turning toward the barn.

"Oh, no you're not." The male EMT grabbed the man by his T-shirt. "You'll be more help if you just stay here with these ladies."

Skye watched the action, running her fingers through her hair, chewing her lip, and coughing. Her stare darted from the scrambling firemen to the shooting flames and billowing smoke to the open door of the barn and back. Soon the tanker at the bottom of the field came racing up, ready with a fresh water supply. But within minutes, the powerful hoses from the first two trucks had put out the flames, and all that seemed damaged on the barn was the one corner and, of course, the damaged hay bales inside.

As the firemen stretched out their now silent hoses, Mr. Chambers, coughing, hurried out of the barn. Mrs. Chambers and Skye, still struggling with their own breaths, rushed to his side.

"Tom, where's Wanda?" Mrs. Chambers could hardly contain herself.

Skye's eyes stung with hot tears and she felt her face flush with fear. "Dad, did you find her?"

Mr. Chambers let out another string of coughs and then struggled to force out his next few words. "She's not in there!"

chapter eight

T hank the Lord," Mrs. Chambers said with a huge
sigh of relief. "But... where could she be?"
Mr. Chambers turned and started hurrying toward
the house. "I'll call the local authorities and ask them to
be on the lookout for Wanda. I'll be right back."

"Maybe she's in town," Skye said to Mrs. Chambers
and Morgan.

"But nothing's open in the wee hours of the night
except the donut shop," Morgan said. "And, somehow, I
don't think Wanda's into donuts."

"I just pray she's okay, wherever she is," Mrs.
Chambers said, her voice cracking.

With the smoke cleared, Mr. and Mrs. Chambers
and Skye checked the barn for further damage while the
firemen checked and re-checked the loft for hot spots.
Then the family rounded up the horses, including an
uncharacteristically compliant Rebel, and put them into
the pasture to continue their morning feast. Thinking
about Wanda through the whole clean-up, Skye found
her own expression matching those of Mr. and Mrs.
Chambers, now draped in constant worry.

At dawn, Mr. Chambers finally had a free moment to call the local police again and see if they had spotted Wanda. With a negative report, he then called Wanda's grandmother and Officer Connors in Harrisburg, alerting them. Then the Chambers' family gathered around the dining room table. Despite the concern for Wanda, all four somehow managed to breathe their first collective sigh of relief in hours. Tippy and Tyler, sensing the drama of the entire situation, lay as close to Mrs. Chambers' feet as they could get.

"Girls," Mr. Chambers said, "We need to pray that God keeps Wanda safe, wherever she is. I also think we need to take time to thank the Lord that no one was hurt and that our barn wasn't destroyed. We lost a few dozen bales of hay, but that was last year's cut. It can easily be replaced with this summer's crop. It looks like I might have to replace a few boards in the loft, too, but first we need to try and figure out what started the fire."

"I'm sure the firemen already have a good idea," Mrs. Chambers said. "I sure hope it's not what I think."

"Like a certain kid named Wanda?" Skye inserted.

"It sure looks suspicious," Mr. Chambers said, "but we can't jump to conclusions."

"And I certainly agree that we need to pray for Wanda and thank God that the fire was put out quickly. It could have been devastating, not only in loss of property but in the loss of our horses. I've been thanking God all morning that you saw that fire when you did, Skye."

"The Lord must have made my mouth dry," Skye said. "I've never been so thirsty, and I felt I just had to get a drink. That's when I spotted the flames."

The family bowed their heads and Mr. Chambers led in prayer. When he finished, Skye looked at everyone as they all sat in silence. Mrs. Chambers, whose blue eyes were flooded with tears, just stared at the table. Mr. Chambers slowly sank down into his chair and crossed his arms. Soot and ash had collected in the fine lines on his face, making him look, for once, as strained and tired as he must have felt. As usual, Morgan's freckled face radiated a generous but weary smile. With their eyes beginning to droop, they all bore the signs of a sleepless night.

"I suppose the first question we need to ask is, 'Where is Wanda?' " Mr. Chambers said.

"And question two is, 'Did she start the fire?' " Skye said.

"There'll be a claims adjuster from the insurance company here sometime this week," Mr. Chambers said. "Then we'll know for sure if someone started it or not."

Mr. Chambers slowly leaned forward in his chair, the events of the night clearly taking their toll. "I really should drive around and see if I can spot Wanda," he said. "She might have hitched a ride in town and be hanging around the mall."

"I sure hope she didn't try anything like that," Mrs. Chambers said, standing. "Hitching a ride with a stranger is so dangerous." She walked into the kitchen. "Tom, please eat something before you leave. We'll all think better on a full stomach. I'll whip up some scrambled eggs. They'll be ready in a few minutes."

Morgan wheeled toward the kitchen. "I'll get the toast and coffee going, Mrs. C."

"And I'd better call the pastor and explain what happened and why we won't be in church this morning," Mr. Chambers said, reaching for the phone on a counter behind him. "We all need a few hours of shut-eye."

Skye went to the cupboard to get four plates and started setting the table. "Mom, where do you think Wanda is? And why did she run?"

"Why did *you* run?" Mrs. Chambers asked.

Skye placed the plates on the table while she thought for a moment. "Mostly because I was scared—even though I tried to act tough."

"Do you think Wanda was brave enough to hitch a ride with someone?" Morgan asked, dumping water into the coffee maker. "Since she's run with a gang for years, I'd have to vote yes. She's probably done a lot more risky things than that in her crazy life."

Mr. Chambers placed the phone back in its cradle and stared out of the sliding door as though his thoughts were in another place, another time. "I noticed on last month's phone bill that someone—who else but Wanda?—has been making phone calls to Harrisburg. My bet is that someone from her gang came and picked her up last night. Whether she left before or after the fire, only time will tell."

R-i-n-g!

The phone rang and Mr. Chambers answered it.

"I see," he finally said. "Yes, please bring her back. We have custody of her for a year. Thank you, sir." Mr. Chambers recited the directions to Keystone Stables, said good-bye, and then hung up the phone.

"Where is she, Tom?" Mrs. Chambers asked, stirring the eggs again. "And is she hurt?"

"Well, it seems like my guess was right. That was Officer Connors from the Harrisburg police department." Mr. Chambers fully relaxed into his chair. "Wanda and a boy named Wheels were just picked up for drunken and disorderly conduct in front of a mini-mart somewhere down there. The boy has a backlog of misdemeanors that are going to keep him busy and off the streets for a few months. Wanda's okay, but—well, Officer Connors said he threatened to put her in juvie hall and throw away the key, and she pleaded with him to let her come back here. Instead of us having to pick her up, they're going to bring her to our door in handcuffs. Officer Connors hopes a long drive in the cage of a police cruiser might help Wanda do a little thinking."

"Hmm, juvie hall or Keystone Stables. The lesser of two evils," Skye joked.

"They'll have her back here in a few hours," Mr. Chambers said.

"Are we going to keep her?" Morgan dropped four slices of bread in the toaster.

"Keystone Stables is a place for second chances," Mrs. Chambers said. "Where would you girls be if we had shipped you out the first time you pulled something?"

"But trying to burn the barn down is serious," Skye said as she placed silverware on the table.

"We can't put the blame on Wanda yet," Mr. Chambers said. "We're not sure what started that fire."

"Well, it sure looks suspicious to me," Skye said.

"Me too," Morgan added. "And we could have lost all our horses. That's dead serious."

"We'll just wait and see what Wanda has to say." Mrs. Chambers carried a bowl of scrambled eggs to the table. "In the meantime, let's eat and try to get some sleep before she gets here—special delivery!"

Everyone released a tired smile, but Skye was sure Wanda wasn't smiling wherever she was.

The ring of the doorbell aroused Skye from a deep sleep. After the fire, she had taken a hot shower, had thrown on clean clothes, and had crashed across her bed. Now she was dreaming about Champ—and Chad—when someone at the front door brought her back to reality.

On her way out of her bedroom, she glanced at her clock. 11:20. In the living room, she joined Mr. and Mrs. Chambers and Morgan, who were lined up along the sofa while Officer Connors "escorted" Wanda in through the door.

Same old Wanda, same old clothes, Skye observed, except this time Wanda's hands were handcuffed behind her back.

"It's good to see you folks again," Officer Connors said as he removed the cuffs from Wanda and clipped them onto his belt. Wanda flopped into the nearest chair she could find, yanked her hat down, and crossed her arms. She didn't say a word.

"This young lady needs to do some growing up," Officer Connors continued. "I know you folks don't have bars on your windows, but it might be a good idea with this gal."

"There'll never be bars on our windows," Mrs. Chambers said, looking at Wanda. "If she can make it for just the remainder of her court order, she may leave, no questions asked. We're just here to help her, but she hasn't accepted that fact yet."

"We're willing to give her a second chance," Mr. Chambers said, "no matter what she's done."

"This place, these people, really helped me," Skye said. "But I had to stop running."

From under her visor, Wanda raised an eyebrow toward Skye but quickly retreated to her former pose.

Morgan beamed a pleasant smile. "I'm sure I'd be in some institution somewhere if they hadn't helped me."

"We love kids," Mrs. Chambers said. "What more can I say?"

"Well, folks, I wish you the best with this one." Officer Connors turned to leave. "She's a tough nut to crack."

Mr. Chambers raised his hand toward the policeman. "One more thing, Officer."

"Yes."

"What time was Wanda apprehended?"

The policeman pushed back his cap and rubbed his forehead. "Let's see—it was about 4:30 this morning. She and Wheels were having a good old time in the parking lot of that mini-mart. Wanda's probably still feeling the effects of her partying. The best thing she could do is sleep it off. Well, gotta be going, and I hope I don't have to see you again." He chuckled as he glanced Wanda's way and hurried out the door.

"Thanks again," Mrs. Chambers said.

"We'll try to stay clear of Harrisburg until the next horse show," Mr. Chambers yelled, shutting the front door. He sat on a chair near Wanda while Mrs. Chambers sat on the sofa. "Morgan," he said, "stay put. Skye, have a seat. This is a family matter, so you're both invited."

Skye sat down and stared at Wanda, who didn't move a muscle.

Mrs. Chambers started. "Wanda—"

Everyone waited for Wanda to look up.

C'mon, Wanda, look at Mom. The words hung on the tip of Skye's tongue. *You can do it.*

Finally Wanda looked up with a scowl on her face that could kill flies.

"We want you to know that we love you, and we're glad you came back," Mrs. Chambers said.

I wonder if anyone ever told her they loved her before, Skye thought.

"But," Mr. Chambers said, "there will be consequences for your actions."

Mrs. Chambers shifted her weight forward on the sofa and folded her hands on her lap. "Wanda, we need to ask you a question, and we need the truth."

Her face empty of all expression, Wanda stared at Mrs. Chambers.

"Did you start the fire?" Mrs. Chambers asked.

The look Wanda gave made it hard for anyone to detect what she was thinking, but her eyes betrayed an element of surprise. "What fire?" she asked with innocence written all over her face.

"The fire in the barn!" Skye blurted out.

"Easy, Skye," Mrs. Chambers said.

Mr. Chambers leaned forward and folded his hands. "Around two thirty this morning, there was a fire in the hayloft of the barn. If Skye hadn't noticed the fire when she got up for a drink, we probably would have lost hundreds of thousands of dollars in property and six very special horses. Were you smoking in the barn again last night?"

Wanda looked down and mumbled, "No."

"We know you've been smoking out there," Morgan said.

Mrs. Chambers said, "Are you *sure* you weren't out there at all last night?"

Wanda sat up in her chair as though someone had poked her with a pin. Her face flushed red and she clenched her fists. "I said I wasn't out there, and I'm telling you the truth. You're just like everybody else. You don't believe me. I didn't start no fire!"

"Then how did it start?" Skye asked while her own face flushed with anger.

"Easy, Skye," Mrs. Chambers gently chided again.

"How should I know?" Wanda spouted. "Wheels picked me up around two o'clock. I wasn't even here at this stupid place all night."

"But the fire started shortly after that," Morgan said.

Wanda launched out of her chair. "I'm telling you, I wasn't near your stupid barn. The last time I was around those stinking horses was yesterday when she made me ride her *precious* Lucy!" Wanda pointed at Mrs. Chambers.

"Wanda," Mr. Chambers said softly, "please sit down. We're not accusing you of anything. We just want to know what happened."

"So," Mrs. Chambers said, "why did you run away?"

Wanda sat with her head down.

"Wanda?" Mrs. Chambers said.

Silence for several more moments. Finally Wanda's glare threw daggers at Mrs. Chambers. "Because I missed my boyfriend, and this place is the pits," she moaned, pulling her hat down over her eyes. A tear trickled down the left side of Wanda's face, and she quickly brushed it away.

"Wanda, we've told you that he can visit you here anytime he wants," Mr. Chambers said. "You are *not* in prison."

"But we do have rules," Mrs. Chambers said. "Wanda—"

This time Wanda looked up at Mrs. Chambers almost immediately.

"We want to—we are going to—believe your story," Mrs. Chambers said, "unless we find out differently. But you will be grounded for two weeks because you used the phone several times without permission and ran away. That means no shooting pool either. Understood?"

Wanda slouched lower into her chair and pulled her arms tight against her chest. "I hate this place," she grumbled, "and the first chance I get, I'm outta here—for good."

chapter nine

Sunday night after church, Mrs. Chambers joined Skye in her bedroom after finishing a short talk with Wanda on the futon and bidding her good night. Mr. Chambers and Morgan were in the dining room playing chess. Skye leaned against the head of her bed while Mrs. Chambers sat at the foot. Tippy and Tyler lay sound asleep on a throw rug near Mrs. Chambers' feet.

"Mom, I think Wanda's telling the truth about the fire," Skye said. "I've thought a lot about the whole situation, and I think she came clean about it."

"What makes you think that?" Mrs. Chambers asked.

"I can just feel it," Skye said. "Remember, I was a kid like that. I can read her pretty good. I don't think she did it."

"We should have a fairly good idea on Tuesday," Mrs. Chambers said. "The insurance company will have a claims adjuster on the scene, and he'll be able to tell us if someone started the fire or not. It shouldn't be too difficult since there wasn't major damage to the barn."

"How's Wanda doing with her schoolwork?"

"She struggles, Skye. But it's not because of her intelligence. She just has no motivation. If she ever makes up her mind to be a better student, she will be. She's satisfied

74

with passing grades and no more. I think her stubborn streak has a lot to do with it."

"I was thinking the other day how I could help her." Skye took a quick glance at her pile of books on her desk and then shifted to Mrs. Chambers. "Although she doesn't want my help — for anything, I think I can get her interested in tackling that English report she has to do."

"What do you have in mind?"

Skye ran her fingers through her hair and explained her plan. "Well, you know how she loves pool. And I know it's just killing her that she can't play for two weeks. Here's my idea. The other day I was online and discovered a website called the WPBA. That stands for the Women's Professional Billiard Association. Mom, you should see all the women who are pro players. The site even had an ESPN TV schedule of all their matches, so last week I watched a final game for a national championship. Wow! Are those women good, and you should see how nice they look. Maybe I can help Wanda in two different ways at the same time."

"Yes, go on." Mrs. Chambers stared at Skye with great interest.

"If Wanda says yes, we can go to that WPBA site on the Internet and then watch a few matches on TV. She can write her composition about the game itself or one of those women. And when she sees how nice those women dress and all, maybe she'll decide to trade her ball cap and Blades jacket for a cool hair style and fancy blouse. What do you think?"

"Now that's a plan!" Mrs. Chambers gave Skye her radiant smile. "Skye, that's a great idea. Her report is due on Friday. Let's see what you two can come up with until then."

Tuesday after school, Skye groomed Champ while waiting impatiently for Wanda and Mrs. Chambers to get home from Maranatha. Morgan had made plans to stay overnight at a friend's home.

After a late supper, Wanda headed to her "quarantined" bedroom, supposedly to do homework. The insurance man had just arrived, and Mr. and Mrs. Chambers were about to escort him to the barn. Skye got permission to visit Wanda, so when the three adults and two dogs left the house, Skye knocked on Wanda's door.

"Yeah, what d'ya want?" Wanda growled.

"It's me," Skye said.

"Go away, horse breath," Wanda snapped. "Whatever you're selling, I'm not interested."

"Wanda, I want to talk to you about pool. C'mon, let me in."

"I can't play pool for two weeks. You know that, so get lost."

"It's not about your playing," Skye said. "It's about professional women pool players."

There was a long pause then Wanda said, "So?"

"Let me in, and I'll explain," Skye pleaded.

Another long moment of silence passed before Wanda finally said, "Awright, awright, come in. But make sure those two fleabags aren't with ya."

Skye went in and leaned against the wall next to the door. Wanda was stretched out in her favorite pose on the bed—hands behind her head and high tops planted firmly into her spread. There wasn't a schoolbook in sight.

"Well?" Wanda blurted out with a sour face.

"Wanda, you're such a good pool player, and I wanted to learn more about the game. So I went online and found the neatest site. It's all about pro women pool players. Did *you* ever check out anything like that online?"

"We don't even have a computer at home," Wanda said.

"I overheard you talking to Mrs. Chambers the other day about a report you had to do, so I was wondering if I could help you write it about female pool players."

Wanda scowled at Skye and then stared at the ceiling. Skye folded her arms and waited.

"I ain't never asked you to do me no favors," Wanda snapped.

"But you'll be doing me a favor," Skye said. "I want to learn more about pool, so while we're writing the paper, you can help me understand the game better."

Wanda stared at the ceiling some more, and Skye just waited.

"When?" Wanda asked.

"I'll ask Mom if we can go online right now."

"Why not?" Wanda said matter-of-factly without moving a muscle.

Skye hurried out of the room and ran to the barn. With permission from Mrs. Chambers, she and Wanda went to one of the computers in the game room and went online to the WPBA website.

While Skye worked the mouse, Wanda slumped in her chair with her arms folded, but her eyes betrayed her passion for the subject on the screen.

"See." Skye pointed at the monitor. "Here's a list of the top ten money-makers from last year. Each one has her own website. This number one rated player, Leona Bushkill, is from England. She made over $100,000 last year. They travel all over the U.S.—well—the world! I had no idea there was that kind of money in playing pool. Did you?"

Wanda peaked her eyebrows, and slowly she sat up in her chair and pulled it closer to the screen.

Skye clicked on Leona Bushkill's name, which opened up the pool player's website. "Last week," Skye said, "I watched this woman play in the U.S. national championship from two years ago. It was on one of the ESPN channels. Did you ever watch any of this stuff at home?"

"We don't have cable either." Wanda huffed.

Skye and Wanda studied everything on the website—poses of Leona at a pool table, her schedule for the remainder of the year, her list of victories since she went pro, and different links with "pool tips."

"I guess since you don't have a computer at home, you don't type." Skye gave Wanda her warmest smile.

"Nope," Wanda said. "I've used computers a few times at school, so I know how to work the mouse and hunt and peck the keyboard, but I can't type my report that way."

"Well, here." Skye pushed the mouse in front of Wanda. "Check out some of these other pool websites while I go get some paper and pencils. We'll take notes, and then you can decide what you want to write your report about."

Wanda took the mouse and dove in. Skye ran upstairs for her supplies and hurried back down. Wanda was completely captivated by the screen and never heard Skye coming.

Skye stood behind Wanda and glanced at a photo on the website of a very attractive thirty-something woman with shoulder-length curly blonde hair and blue eyes.

"Wow! Who's that?" Skye said. "She's gorgeous."

"That babe is Gretchen Cummings, and she's from Sweden." Wanda's voice, now an octave higher than normal, almost screeched with excitement. "She's won four world championships, two in Snooker, and two in Nine Ball. I ain't never played Snooker."

Skye sat down next to Wanda and for the next hour they surfed the web, visiting the websites of a handful of female pool players. Skye noticed, along with some very interesting facts about each of the players, that almost every one of them made a distinguishable feminine appearance. It was time for Skye to make a point.

"Wanda," Skye said as she made notes, "what do you notice about all these women?"

"They're experts!" Wanda said. "But they all say that they practice from 30 to 50 hours a week. I guess it takes that much time at the table to be a pro."

"But how about the way they look?" Skye held up her hand and touched her five fingers. "Every one of those last five looks really pretty with her hair styled just right. What do you think?"

Wanda shrugged while she glared at the screen. "Guess so."

Skye glanced at the screen and pointed. "Now look at this one. Kim Mau Yang. She's from the Philippines. Look at her cool long black hair. It's so clean, it almost sparkles. And I've noticed something else about all of these pool women."

"What?" Wanda asked.

"They all wear nice clothes, make-up, and jewelry. They all look so cool. A few weeks ago I saw a championship match about ten years old, and the one women was wearing a black evening gown all the way down to the floor."

Wanda scrunched up her face. "Shooting pool in a dress? No way!"

"Honest," Skye said. "I could hardly believe it myself. But I think that is so cool, because when the average bear like me thinks of pool, do you know what I think of right away? It's a 'man's sport.' But to see women playing pool and looking so feminine and pretty is awesome to me. I just think that's really neat. What do you think?"

Wanda simply said, "Guess so."

Behind the girls, the basement door opened, and Skye turned.

"Hi, Mom," Skye said while Wanda stayed glue to the screen.

"Girls, the insurance man just gave us his full report." Mrs. Chambers walked to the girls and stood behind them. She placed a hand on each of the girl's shoulders. Wanda shrugged, and Mrs. Chambers pulled her hand away.

Mrs. Chambers continued. "He said the fire started from a bad wire. It must have frayed and set off sparks that caught the hay on fire."

"Told ya I didn't do it," Wanda declared without ever looking away from the computer.

"Guess so," Skye said, smiling.

chapter ten

Skye, try working Rebel in the opposite direction." Chad stood a short distance away from the corral and threw training tips at Skye. "Maybe he's left-hoofed," he said with a chuckle.

It was a cloudy but warm Saturday afternoon in May, and Skye was in the middle of another session with "the stubborn mule." She backed away and withdrew the rope she had been using to prompt the horse to circle toward his right. As usual, she walked to the opposite side of the corral and turned her back to the horse, waiting for him to come to her. And, as usual, Rebel pivoted his body, faced his tail at Skye and arched his neck over the fence.

Skye slowly approached the horse, whirling her rope and forcing Rebel to trot to his left. As Skye concentrated, she heard Wanda yelling Chad's name from the backyard and coming closer—fast! Out of the corner of her eye, Skye spotted Wanda, who looked strangely different.

"Chad, ole buddy," Wanda chimed. "How about a game of pool?"

"Oh, hi, Wanda," Chad said as Wanda rubbed shoulders with him. "Wow! I see you have a new look."

New look? What's she up to now? Skye quickly coiled the rope in her hands and slipped between the fence rails. The new Wanda faced her, eyeball to eyeball.

Skye clenched her jaw, determined not to let her face betray any hint of surprise. Her glance darted to Chad, who stood rolling his eyes behind Wanda.

Wanda certainly had a new look, and Skye wondered how much of it had to do with her visit to the pool players' website earlier in the week. *And I wonder if Mom knows what she looks like. I'm sure she does.*

Skye studied every inch of Wanda from head to toe. First, Wanda had a new hairdo, a deliberate spike job. But she had used so much mousse, stiff spikes stood out all over her head like the Statue of Liberty. Adorning her ears were long dangling sparkly earrings, the clip-on kind that Mrs. Chambers had probably worn at some black-tie affair twenty years ago. Then there was Wanda's face, literally "covered" in make-up. Her cheeks glowed like two ripe tomatoes, and her eyes, lined and shadowed in deep purple, looked like some dead Egyptian queen's. Worse yet, she topped them off with obnoxiously fake eyelashes.

Skye's stare drifted to Wanda's clothes, which were all brand-new. *But nothing matches!*

Wanda sported a frilly pink "Sunday" blouse, designer blue jeans, and low-cut white sneakers. From her neck down, Wanda didn't look half bad other than the gaudy costume jewelry. Four strands of sparkly rhinestones hugged her neck, and on each wrist an excess of bracelets dangled in mismatched, clashing colors. *More of Mom's ancient treasures*, Skye mused.

"Where'd you get the new duds?" Chad asked.

"The woman bought them for me when I first moved in," Wanda said, pointing toward the house and batting her eyelashes at Chad. "I just decided to wear them today."

"I see." Chad tried his best to be cordial. "Interesting."

"So, Wanda," Skye said, "how come we have a new you?"

"Just because." Wanda snapped at Skye and then turned to Chad. "How about that pool game now, Chad?"

Chad looked like he didn't know quite what to say. "Ah—not right now, Wanda. I promised Skye that I'd work with her all afternoon with Rebel and the other horses. Sorry. I'm tied up for the next few hours. Maybe after supper."

Skye stared at Wanda's earrings and struggled to hold in a laugh that pressed against her lips. "You never told me how you did on your report. Didn't you give that to Mom yesterday?"

Wanda stared at Chad and tried to ignore Skye. "Yeah, but she didn't grade it yet. Chad, don'tcha have time for just one game now?"

"Well—"

"Did Mom tell you that for supper we're having a picnic at the pavilion?" Skye said to Wanda. "Dad and Morgan are cooking burgers and baked potatoes on the grill."

"Yeah, she told me." Wanda gave Skye a sour look and started walking toward the house. "Big deal."

"Maybe later, Wanda. Okay?" Chad called after her.

Without another word, Wanda hurried back into the house.

For the rest of the afternoon, Skye and Chad worked with Rebel and took a few breaks in between. On one break, they went into the barn to check on Mr. Chambers' progress with his clean-up job. Another time they got a drink of lemonade and sat at the gazebo and talked about everything and about nothing. By now, the clouds had parted and the brilliant spring sun bathed the place in a blanket of warmth. When Skye was with Chad, she felt as warm on the inside as she did on the out. She hoped he felt the same.

"I wonder what Wanda's been doing all afternoon," Chad said to Skye as they walked back to the training corral.

"When I went inside for our lemonade," Skye said, "the new Wanda was sitting at the dining room table doing schoolwork. It's my bet that Mom discovered some unfinished assignments, so Wanda probably got her thousandth lecture. Even though she's grounded for another week, Mom and Dad still will let her come to the picnic. That way they can keep an eye on her."

"Right now, with the way she looks, that's pretty easy to do. She's hard to miss," Chad said. "I don't mean that in a nasty way, but I hope she doesn't go to church like that tomorrow. I know a couple of kids who'll laugh right in her face."

"Yeah, I do, too," Skye said. "I sure didn't want to laugh at her and hurt her feelings, but it wasn't easy. I'm sure Mom will tone down Wanda's looks a little."

"Skye!" Mrs. Chambers yelled from the back door of the house. "We're going to start carrying things out to the pavilion for the picnic. Would you and Chad help us, please?"

"Sure, Mom!" Skye yelled back. "I'll put Rebel out to pasture, and then I'll be right there."

Chad started toward the house. "I'm on my way, Mrs. C."

"Chad, can you get the gates for me first?" Skye grabbed her rope off a fence post and walked on the outside of the training corral toward Rebel.

"Oh, sure," Chad answered. "No problem."

Skye carefully approached Rebel who stood in his favorite position, head arched out over the top rail. She snuck her hand underneath his chin and clipped the rope unto the halter. Then, with Rebel on the inside and her on the outside, she led him to where Chad was slowly opening the gate.

"Easy, boy," she said as the pinto slipped out of the corral and pranced in circles. As Chad quietly closed the gate, Skye led Rebel, snorting like an engine, toward the large fenced-in pasture where the rest of the horses were grazing at the bottom near the pond. Chad hurried ahead of her, unlatched the gate and swung it open.

At the opened gate, one careful step at a time, Skye approached the horse, slowly moved her hand toward his halter, and unsnapped the rope. Just as Rebel started into the field, a loud noise echoed from the barn, like two boards slapping together, and Rebel reared with a loud neigh.

"Easy, boy!" Skye said.

The horse's eyes bulged with fright as he reared again and pivoted toward the open gate.

"Whoa, Rebel!" Chad said, raising his hands, but it was too late.

Rebel charged out of the pasture and along the fence toward the picnic grove. Full speed ahead, he rounded the corner, high-tailed it down the dirt road, and in a cloud of dust disappeared into the thickest woods.

"Rebel!" Skye yelled at the top of her lungs. "Come back here!"

W e've got to find that horse before dark," Skye said to Chad and Mr. Chambers as they trailed Rebel through the back ten acres of Keystone Stables. "If he wanders on other farmlands or open fields, he'll run like the wind and we'll never catch him."

"Well, we're not going to catch him if we stay together," Mr. Chambers said, glancing at his watch. "We've got to split up to cover the five different paths leading to Piney Hollow. Chad, you take the east trail, and Skye, you cover the two center trails. I'll check out the west end. Let's meet in an hour at the campsite. If you see him, we can form our posse again and try to round him up."

"Okay, Mr. C.," Chad said, reining his mount to his left. "See you both in an hour."

"And I hope one of us will have a good report," Skye said, riding straight ahead on a path into thickening woods.

Mr. Chambers reined his horse to the right. "One hour then — at Piney Hollow!"

As Skye rode Champ through the woods, she started sharing her heart, just as she had done so many times

85

before with her best horse friend. "You know, Champ, this is as good a time as any to talk out some of my problems," Skye said, stroking her horse's bobbing neck, "Rebel and Wanda are so much alike, it's unreal."

Champ nickered while he twitched his ears free of buzzing flies.

"I want to help them both, but neither of them will give me one second of their time. What am I doing wrong?"

The squeaking saddle and jangling bridle took Skye through thick woods where she searched as far as her eye could see, but in vain. When the hour had passed, she headed toward Piney Hollow, but with a new plan for Wanda.

Riding into the clearing, Skye spotted Mr. Chambers and Chad sitting on wooden crates next to the chuck wagon, chewing on long strands of field grass.

They're probably wishing Mom were out here with some grilled food, Skye thought, glancing at her watch. "6:50," Skye said to Champ. "I'm starved too."

"Hey, Skye!" Chad yelled as soon as he spotted her. "Any sign of him?"

"Not a hair!" Skye yelled back. She rode to the hitching rail, dismounted Champ, and joined her dad and Chad.

R-i-n-g!

Yanking his cell phone from his shirt pocket, Mr. Chambers flipped it open. "Hello? No, Hon, we didn't sight him. We'll stay out another hour yet. Keep the home fires burning. Love ya. See you soon. Bye." He flipped the phone shut and stuck it back in his pocket.

"Dad, where are we going to look next? I'm hungry," Skye said.

"You're hungry?" Mr. Chambers joked, pointing his thumb over his shoulder. "I'm hungry enough to chew on that wagon wheel. But, let's give our search one more go. We'll ride over the ridge to Garsides' farm and see if we can spot Rebel in any of the open fields. If not, we'll head

86

back and start again tomorrow after church. There's not much more we can do now. It would be super if he'd wander back home and save us a lot of time and trouble."

"He is *some* horse," Chad said. "Somehow I don't think he'll come home on his own."

Mr. Chambers glanced at his watch. "We'll only stay out another hour and then head back. It'll be almost dark when we get home."

Skye pulled a long strand of wild grass, stuck it between her lips and giggled again. "Maybe I'll try some of this wild stuff too. That should hold me over." She chewed a couple of times and then deadpanned, "Hey, what do you know? I'm feeling full already."

The other two laughed as Mr. Chambers stood. "Well, we need to get moving."

"Dad?" Skye said.

"Yes, Skye. What is it?"

"Could we pray about this whole mess? I've been doing some thinking, and have you noticed how Rebel and Wanda are so much alike?"

"Why, they're almost twins," Chad joked. "Except for their hairdos."

"I think I've been trying too hard to help the both of them," Skye said, "and it's not working."

Mr. Chambers sat down, leaned his elbows on his knees, and folded his hands. "Sure we can pray about finding Rebel—and helping Wanda. But what do you mean that you're trying too hard?"

"I keep thinking of the horse training camp that Chad and I went to last summer. Our mentor kept telling us that, before we win the horse over to our side, we have to let him decide to accept us as the leader of his 'herd.' We can't force him to bond with us. We can only give him the choice. I don't think I've been giving Rebel enough time to make up his mind."

"And what about Wanda?" Chad asked.

Skye folded her arms and stared off into the blue sky dotted with whipped-cream clouds. "I think I'm going to try something new with my foster sister."

"Which is—" Chad said.

"Girl whispering," Skye said.

"Hmm," Mr. Chambers said. "Interesting concept. When we get back to the house, I'd like to hear more of your idea. Well, let's pray and we'll get moving."

The three bowed their heads as Mr. Chambers led in a heartfelt prayer about Wanda, Rebel, and the overall Keystone Stables ministry. When the prayer had finished, Skye looked straight ahead and froze at what she saw near the tree line about a half football field's length away.

"Sh-h," she whispered, "and don't even blink."

GARROU, ELISABETH GRACE

Unclaim : 01/22/2023

Held date   : 01/14/2023
Pickup location : Beaverton Murray Scholls

Title   : Whispering hope
Call number   : J HUBLER, Marsha #007
Item barcode   : 33614046502398
Assigned branch : Hillsboro Brookwood Library

Notes:

t's Rebel," Skye whispered. "He just walked out of the woods and is feasting on the field grass. I'm not sure he sees us."

"He *has* to see the other horses," Mr. Chambers whispered as both he and Chad slowly turned to look. "But he might not have connected them with us. It's my guess that he'll mosey on over this way to see if he knows any of them personally."

"What should we do, Mr. C.?" Chad whispered.

"First I need to get my rope off my saddle." Mr. Chambers paused. "Chad, I want you to sneak around the back of the chuck wagon and make your way across the left side of the field. Crawl if you have to and try to get about thirty feet from him. Skye, you go to the right along the tree line and try to get about the same distance from him on that side."

"What if he sees me?" Skye whispered.

"That's okay, because if he decides to move, I think it will be in this direction toward the other horses. Just walk real slow. Now wait until I get my rope before you both move. I'm going to hide behind those trees." He pointed to a cluster of pines near the horses. "Chad, when Skye gets even with you on the other side of the field, stand up. Then both of you take turns talking softly to him. Slowly start walking toward him and try to coax him this way. If nothing spooks him back into the woods, he should come close enough for me to lasso him. I think his urge to join with our horses will be in our favor."

Skye and Chad waited until Mr. Chambers carefully retrieved his rope and crept behind the trees. Then they separated and made their way at a slug's pace along the perimeter of the field, sandwiching Rebel in between.

When Skye had advanced about half way, Rebel suddenly lifted his head. He arched his neck, pitched his ears toward Skye, and let out a series of snorts. His gorgeous black-and-white mane and tail whisked in a gentle breeze. Skye froze on the spot. Rebel stared straight at her, pranced forward a few steps and snorted again. After one loud whinny, he appeared to decide that Skye was no threat. He lowered his head and went back to his graze.

On the left side of the field, Chad snuck to his destination and waited for Skye. As she moved to her spot, Rebel again arched his neck and watched every move Skye made.

"Hey, Rebel," Skye said softly. "Easy, boy. It's time to go home now."

"Easy, fella." Chad stood and started moving in on Rebel's other side. "No one's going to hurt you."

Rebel turned sharply toward Chad and let out another snorting blast. Skye could see every muscle in the pinto's powerful body tense and ripple as he stared in Chad's direction.

Skye took a few steps forward. "Easy, boy."

The horse shifted his body back toward Skye. With another loud neigh, he pranced several steps toward the pines where Mr. Chambers had hidden. Again, Skye and

Chad moved forward on each of Rebel's flanks, forcing him in the direction of the trees.

All of a sudden, Rebel reared up on his hind legs, released another loud whinny, and charged across the field.

"Dad," Skye yelled, backtracking a few yards, "here he comes!"

"Get him, Mr. C.!" Chad yelled.

Skye watched as Mr. Chambers moved just a short distance away from the trees and prepped his lasso. As far as she could tell, he was completely hidden from Rebel's view.

Mr. Chambers started to whirl his rope and waited.

Rebel tore across the field, oblivious to what was straight ahead.

Chad came running to Skye's side. "Man, that horse is fast," he said. "Look at him go!"

"And Dad's got only one chance to rope him. If he misses, Rebel will be long gone into the woods, probably into the next county."

Rebel galloped full speed ahead, right toward the trees.

Mr. Chambers firmly planted both feet and patiently whirled the lasso.

"Rebel doesn't see him yet, does, he?" Chad puffed.

"Nope," Skye answered.

Rebel ran like he was heading for a finish line, still unaware of Mr. Chambers and his trap.

"So far so good," Skye said.

Closer, even closer, Rebel ran.

Closer...

"Now!" Chad and Skye yelled in unison.

Skye gnawed her lip as she watched Mr. Chambers launch his rope and release a large loop into the air. The lasso floated for a few seconds. Then, almost as if guided by an invisible hand, the loop slipped over the head of the charging horse. The rope tightened around Rebel's neck, and the horse came to an abrupt skidding stop.

"He got him!" Skye yelled.

Mr. Chambers dug his heels into the ground and pulled with all his strength. While he ran around one of the pines and tightened his tether, Rebel threw an absolute wild-horse fit! He bucked and reared and squealed, but the more he bucked and reared, the tighter and shorter his tether became. The sturdy pine would not give an inch.

As Skye and Chad ran toward Mr. Chambers, she shifted her glance to Champ and the other two horses, still tied to the rail. Aroused by the commotion, they started to whinny, sidestep and stomp, doing their best to join the action. But their reins held secure.

"Way to go, Dad!" Skye cried, focusing on Rebel.

"Nice going, Mr. C.!" Chad said. "That was some lasso demonstration!"

Mr. Chambers was still clutching his end of the rope near the tree while Rebel pulled and squealed. Mr. Chambers took off his Stetson and wiped his forehead with his arm. "I think I had some divine intervention!" He wound the rope around the tree again and knotted the rope. "It's been ten years since I lassoed a bronco as fast as this one." He stepped in front of Rebel and raised his hand. "Easy, Reb," he said. "Calm down now. It's all over."

Skye studied the wild Mustang's antics, and it seemed to her as though the horse actually understood that his plight was in vain. With one quick whinny he stopped pulling, stood firm, snorted at his audience, and went back to grazing as if not a thing had happened. In the early evening sun, his black-and-white body almost sparkled from the oozing sweat.

"Wow, he is one gorgeous hunk," Skye said then turned toward Champ and the other horses, who were still spooked. She ran to Champ and grabbed his halter, calming him down. In seconds, the other horses followed suit. "Okay, guys, the show is over," she said, stroking Champ's neck. "You'll soon be back in your stalls with a double portion of oats."

"I hope I get a double portion of chow too," Chad said as he joined her.

Mr. Chambers walked to his horse and patted its neck. "We all get double portions tonight," he said.

"Hay or oats?" Chad joked.

"Burgers," Mr. Chambers said.

"And hold the field grass, please," Skye said, giggling.

After Skye and her posse brought Rebel back to Keystone Stables, the three gorged themselves on Mrs. Chambers' and Morgan's gourmet picnic food. Chad stayed for several more hours, and the "new" Wanda tried her best to grab his attention, to no avail. Still grounded from pool table action, she decided to play "boring" dominoes with the rest of the family while staring holes through Chad.

When Chad left at ten o'clock, Wanda declared with a string of obnoxious yawns that she wanted to go to bed. After family devotions that Wanda managed to tolerate, she went downstairs to sleep on the futon. Mr. and Mrs. Chambers sat at the dining room table with Skye and Morgan. They discussed school matters, the recent barn fire, and Rebel and his latest antics. Finally, the conversation led to Wanda and how they all could help her.

"Mom," Skye said, "are you going to let her go to church looking like she did today? I know most of the kids will just shrug her off, but there are a few girls that could really be nasty and say something to hurt her."

"I'll do my best to tone down her appearance," Mrs. Chambers said. "I'm hoping she'll listen. She really is quite an attractive young lady. She just needs to learn how to look and act like one. We'll work on it."

"I hope she listens to you, Mrs. C.," Morgan said. "Some of those girls in the youth group can be mean. Wanda doesn't need any of that dumped on her yet."

"I think I'll call George and his wife tomorrow morning," Mr. Chambers said. "Depending on how Wanda looks, it might be a good idea to warn them ahead of time. Maybe they can ward off any potential trouble in the Youth for Truth class."

"Good idea," Mrs. Chambers said. "And I'll try to do my part on this end of things."

"Mom, do you know that Wanda has terrible nightmares?" Skye asked. "Because she sleeps right beneath my room, I can hear her yelling right through the floor!"

"I know about her bad dreams, honey," Mrs. Chambers said. "We heard her after she first moved in. I look for her to soon open up in her counseling sessions at Maranatha so we can get to the root of her troubles. She'd feel better about a lot of things if she'd just talk them out."

"I know when she starts trusting us, she'll start talking," Skye said.

"So, Skye," Mr. Chambers said, "tell me more about your 'girl whispering' idea that you shared with me at Piney Hollow today."

"Girl whispering?" Mrs. Chambers said. "This should be interesting."

Morgan eased out a warm smile and pushed her hair behind her shoulders. "I would think that Wanda has gotten nothing her whole life but 'girl yelling.'"

"I keep thinking of what Chad and I learned last summer at that horse whispering camp," Skye said. "Our mentor kept telling us over and over not to force ourselves on the horse. I think that's what I've been doing—not just with Rebel but with Wanda too. I'd like to be her friend, but she wants to stay a zillion miles away."

"She's a totally hard nut to crack." Morgan nodded, her freckles dancing with her signature smile.

"So, what's your plan?" Mr. Chambers leaned back in his chair and folded his arms. "I'm all ears."

Mrs. Chambers grabbed a pretzel from the bowl and took a bite. "At this point in time, we need God's wisdom to help Wanda. What's on your mind, Skye?"

"I remember how I was when I first came here," Skye said. "I didn't trust anyone because so many people had broken promises to me or they had just let me down. I wanted to have friends, but I didn't want to risk being hurt all over again like I had been in the past. I think that's what's going on with Wanda."

"I think you're absolutely right," Mrs. Chambers said. "We have to win her confidence, but it'll take time. And she has to be willing to try, as well. So far, she's not done anything but buck the system."

"Just like Rebel," Morgan said. "Always *bucking* the system."

Everyone chuckled while Mr. Chambers said, "That's a good one, Morgan. Very good."

"Anyway," Skye continued, "I've been thinking about how Morgan treated me when I first moved in. In a way, she was 'girl whispering' with me, and we didn't know it."

"What do you mean?" Morgan's freckled face lit up with another big smile.

"Well, do you remember how you offered to help me with my homework, and you said you wanted to be my friend, but then you backed away and didn't push it? You went on with your life, enjoying every minute, and you weren't going to let me ruin it. After awhile, I couldn't stand it anymore. I wanted to find out what made you click and enjoy things like you did, so I started coming around. Remember?"

"Kinda," Morgan said. "I do remember you asking me how I could enjoy life in this wheelchair. That blew your mind. Another thing I remember is that you were also a totally tough nut to crack."

"Ahem," Mrs. Chambers teased, looking Morgan straight in the eye. "Speaking of totally tough nuts to crack..."

"Maybe we should be playing 'The Nutcracker Suite' on a CD," Mr. Chambers joked, and everyone laughed. Then his tone changed. "Seriously, Skye, what do you have in mind for Wanda?"

"It's simple," Skye said. "I don't want to be nasty to her, and I'm not going to ignore her, but I'm just going to be polite and go about my business. Maybe when she stands back and takes a good look at how happy I am—really, how happy we all are—she'll want to be part of it. What do you think?" Skye looked around the table.

"Anything's worth a try," Mr. Chambers said.

"Just let me know if there's any progress between you two," Mrs. Chambers said.

"Go for it," Morgan said. "We might just begin to see another nut getting totally cracked!"

Sunday morning, the Chambers family attended church. Although Mrs. Chambers tried to tone down Wanda's looks, Skye thought Wanda still managed to look like a scared porcupine. Fortunately, Hannah Gilbert and Betty Feaster weren't in class, so as far as Skye could tell, all Wanda got were a few quizzical looks from the other kids.

After the Chambers family enjoyed a roast beef dinner at Keystone Stables, Skye waited for Chad to arrive. At one o'clock, the two headed to the training corral with Rebel while Mr. and Mrs. Chambers read the paper in the living room and Morgan and Wanda did schoolwork at the dining room table.

From the start, as Skye led Rebel out of the barn, she sensed something different. *Is it with Rebel or me?* she pondered. *Maybe it's my confidence in my new plan!*

"Chad," Skye said as she released Rebel into the corral, "I was thinking that maybe I should try the same technique on Rebel that I've been planning for Wanda. I have to take my time and not be so forceful—with either of them."

"Sounds like a plan, Skye. Go for it," Chad said, closing the gate behind Skye. He then stood back and watched.

Rebel, as usual, had already trotted to the opposite side of the corral and had reached his head out over the fence, his whisking tail facing Skye.

"Here we go, Rebel, boy," Skye said softly, walking to the center of the corral. Carefully she started twirling her rope, forcing the horse to trot around the perimeter of the pen. After a few laps, Skye reversed Rebel's direction, running him a few more minutes before allowing him to stop. "Okay, Rebel," Skye said coiling her rope in her hands, "that was real good."

For a moment, Rebel stood in place, staring at Skye while he puffed to catch his breath. Then, as expected, he pivoted and resumed his normal pose, head over the rail, tail toward Skye.

"What a rascal!" Skye said as she spun around and walked toward the fence on her side of the corral, turning her back toward the horse. "Chad," she said softly, "I'm going to stay here as long as it takes until he moves. Let me know what he's doing."

"You bet," Chad said. They both stood and waited.

And waited ...

Rebel seemed perfectly content gazing at the horses far down in the pasture and completely ignoring Skye. But then, after about ten minutes…

"He just looked at you, Skye," Chad said. "Be cool."

Skye stared at the back of the house. Inside at the sliding door, Wanda was looking out.

"He's turning toward you," Chad said as Rebel pivoted his body and faced Skye. Skye nonchalantly glanced to her side, watching Rebel's every move out of the corner of her eye.

Skye watched Rebel as he released a loud whinny and nodded, his long, flowing mane bobbing with every move. Practically begging for attention, he whinnied again and pawed the ground.

Skye stood firm.

"Here he comes," Chad whispered.

Skye listened as one hoof beat at a time, Rebel came toward her. She inched her way to the fence, leaned her arms on the rail, and looked the other way.

Slowly, Rebel came closer …

And closer …

Rebel stopped, pawed the ground again, and let out a string of anxious snorts. He was so close now that Skye felt his steamy breath billowing against the back of her neck.

"He's about three feet away," Chad whispered. "Don't move."

chapter fourteen

With a horse as damaged as Rebel, Skye wasn't sure what he might do next. He could rear up, or he could try to run. But just maybe ...

"Don't move," Chad said. "He's reaching toward you."

Skye waited ...

Another minute passed.

Finally, the horse's muzzle nudged her arm and he released a friendly nicker.

"Easy, Skye," Chad whispered.

Skye released a sigh of relief and slowly turned toward the horse. Rebel stretched toward her, his lips starting to nibble her sleeve. Inching her hand toward the horse, she finally stroked the horse's beautiful black-and-white face.

"Good boy, Rebel," she said softly. "We've done it. We're going to be good friends, aren't we?" She took one careful step to the horse's side and reached up, stroking his tense arched neck. Softly, he nickered again and then seemed to release his own sigh of relief while Skye clipped the rope to his halter and stroked his muzzle again.

Slowly Chad approached, gingerly leaned on the fence, and whispered his next few words. "Skye, you've done it. He's finally given in and bonded with you."

"And he'll find out it's much better to be with us than against us." Skye gave Chad a victorious smile. "I think he's decided to trust us. In no time we'll be saddling him and riding him on the trail."

When her grounding ended, Wanda spent every minute of her spare time at her favorite spot—the pool table. Of course, she had to keep up her schoolwork and do her regular chores first, which she always did with a double portion of griping. Then she made a beeline for the game room.

As far as her new appearance, she decided to keep her porcupine look after several other clients at Maranatha thought she looked cool, but the make-up and jewelry were just too much trouble, so she parked those items next to her school books, in a corner of her bedroom and out of sight.

Skye and Morgan had initiated Skye's girl-whispering plan with Wanda all week long but had not noticed any significant change in Wanda's attitude or actions. She went on her merry nasty way, engrossed in her own misery and pain.

Patience and tough love, my dear, Skye remembered Chad saying a while back. Yes, she figured while working on a report at a computer one evening, getting through to the gangbanger was going to take some time. While Wanda played pool by herself, Morgan played "Battleship" at a computer next to Skye.

"Skye, what's your report about?" Morgan was busy with her game controls.

"Well," Skye stopped typing and stared at the screen, "believe it or not, I'm writing a paper about the game of pool for science class."

"You and pool?" Morgan's voice raised an octave. "I didn't think you were that interested in the game."

"Well, I wasn't until Wanda moved in," Skye said.

For a brief moment Wanda stopped shooting, and the room grew silent. Skye figured, and hoped, that Wanda was eavesdropping on their conversation. Disregarding Wanda's interest, Skye continued talking to Morgan. "When I helped her with a report a few weeks ago, I really got interested in the technical stuff. Morgan, did you know that if someone is good at geometry, he or she would be good at pool?"

"How so?" Morgan said, staring at her screen.

Skye faced Morgan, and out of the corner of her eye, she could see Wanda pretending to analyze a shot at the table. *It's taking too long for her to shoot,* Skye reasoned. *She's got to be listening.*

"Pool is a game of angles," Skye said. "On this one website, they show you all this neat stuff about making shots and how you have to hit the balls and use the cushions and all. Did you ever hear this geometry rule: 'The angle of incidence equals the angle of reflection'?"

"Yeah, I just had that in my geometry course a few lessons ago," Morgan said. "That's really cool that you found all that stuff about the game."

Out of the corner of her eye, Skye saw Wanda walking toward her. "Hi, Wanda," Skye said nonchalantly, turning back to the computer.

"What'd ya just say about pool?" Wanda grumbled.

"Oh, not much." Skye typed away. "I'm writing a report about it. That's all."

Morgan had nothing to say.

Wanda stood behind Skye for a moment and then returned to her pool game.

Skye typed a few more sentences and then said to Morgan, "Did you know there are different sized tables, different kinds of balls and different kinds of cloths for the table? All those things affect the angles and how fast the balls go."

"Didn't know that," Morgan said.

"Oh, and get this. The pool sticks are different lengths and weights. A heavy stick weighs about 20 ounces or more. All that stuff is important to know if you want to be a champion pool player."

"Cool," Morgan said.

Pecking away, Skye listened as Wanda shot two more balls then walked to the computer station and, again, stood behind Skye. Skye kept typing, and Morgan played her game.

"My stick's a Brunswick 18 ouncer," Wanda said.

"What's that?" Skye kept typing.

"I'm talking about my pool stick. It weighs 18 ounces and was made by Brunswick, one of the best billiard companies. It was first prize in the junior pool tournament I won last year."

"That's nice," Morgan said.

Skye kept typing. "I have to get this report done by Monday. I want to put some stuff in it about some of the women pros I found on the web. They are so cool."

"What's so neat about them?" Morgan asked.

"Well, for one thing," Skye said, "they're from all over the world. I emailed one of them from California who was a world champ about ten years ago, but she's retired now. She emailed me back and told me she's a Christian! She also told me that she goes around the country giving 'Gospel Trick Shot' exhibitions and then talks about Jesus at the end of her show. That's unreal."

"Now that is too cool," Morgan said.

Skye continued, "Some of these pool women are married, and—oh, you're gonna love this—last week I watched a match, and the one player, Linda Lou Carvell, was pregnant! Now how many sports are there where a pregnant woman can compete and maybe even become a champ?"

"No way!" Wanda blurted out. "She had one in the hangar and was shooting pool?" She flopped in an empty chair next to Skye. "Go to her website, and let's see what she has on there."

This is good. Skye glanced at Morgan whose eyes were saying the same thing.

"Don't you want to finish your pool game?" Skye asked Wanda.

"Later." Wanda pointed at Skye's screen. "I wanna see this Linda babe. Maybe she'll have a picture on there showing her shooting pool in her *condition.*"

Skye looked at Morgan, gave her a sly smile, and peaked her eyebrows.

Morgan lowered her hand to her side and gave Skye a thumbs-up.

"Okay, Wanda," Skye said. "Let me finish this part of my report, and we'll surf the web and look for some WPBA sites."

Wanda pulled her chair closer to the station and stared at the screen. "I guess if I'm going to be a pro billiard player, I need to learn more about the competition."

"We'll be glad to help," Morgan said. "Just ask."

"I wouldn't be sitting here if I wasn't asking now," Wanda snapped.

I think she's starting to trust us, Skye thought as she returned a hidden thumbs-up to Morgan. *We should be friends in no time at all.*

y the end of May, Rebel and Wanda were making dramatic progress. Because of Skye and everyone else at Keystone Stables, *both* rebels were feeling real love for the first time in their lonely, wounded lives.

Skye considered Morgan not only her foster sister but also her best friend, and she loved to hang out with her in Morgan's bedroom when they both had free time. On a rainy Sunday afternoon, Skye joined Morgan and they discussed school, Chad, the youth group, Chad, and finally Wanda and Rebel. While Morgan sat in her Jazzy near a desk, Skye flopped on her back across the bed.

"Morgan," Skye said, "do you realize that through all the prayer and hard work we've put in, two miracles were happening right before our eyes?"

Morgan glanced at the window that had streams of water cascading over it like a waterfall. Thunder rumbled in the distance. "You got it, Skye. I think Rebel's days of bucking the system are over. Wasn't it only a week after your breakthrough that you could saddle and bridle him?"

"Yep," Skye answered. "And he absolutely loves when I groom him and give him apples. He's not doing too bad with his hoof cleaning either. He's learning not to pull away when I want to pick up his foot. He'll conquer that fear in no time."

"I was watching from the dining room when you first slipped on his back a few weeks ago, and that was awesome! He walked around that corral like he had been doing it since he was born."

"And did you see Chad working with him too? As soon as Rebel bonded with me, it was like he wasn't afraid of anyone at all. He lets Chad tack him and ride him and everything."

"Skye, I think we can say that Rebel is now an official member of the Keystone Stables equine family."

"We sure can, sis," Skye said.

"Then there's Wanda," Morgan said as she straightened a messy pile of schoolbooks on her desk.

"That has shocked me more than Rebel!" Skye said. "The biggest change I've noticed is Wanda's attitude about church. I don't know if she's accepted Christ yet, but have you seen how she actually sits up straight and pays attention to the Sunday school lessons and sermons in the main services?"

"Yep," Morgan said, spinning her wheelchair toward the bed. "And how about the way she's acting at home? I think it's super."

"Well, all week long she was on kitchen duty, and I didn't hear one gripe. She pitched a sour face Mom's way only once in a while about her homework and chores, and she was doing them without being asked a zillion times."

"Have you found any butts lying around?" Morgan asked.

"Nope, and have you noticed her Blades duds have been missing lately? I think she's actually proud that she goes to Maranatha the way she wears that sweatshirt all the time."

"And the other night at supper, remember she even laughed at somebody's dumb joke," Morgan added with a big smile. "Now that's definitely change!"

It was time for the Youth for Truth to come for another party! On the last Thursday in May, the Keystone Stables clan was already busy making plans for Saturday afternoon when the teens would arrive for a picnic, horseback riding, billiards, and other games. When Mr. and Mrs. Chambers and Morgan decided to check out the gazebo and pavilion, Wanda asked Skye if she'd like to shoot some pool. Without a second thought, Skye said yes. She believed that it was time for her to park her girl-whispering technique in a corner somewhere and try to gain Wanda's confidence once and for all.

In their fifth game, Wanda shot the nine ball into a corner pocket, giving her a five-game sweep. "Hey, horse breath, can I talk to you?" Wanda said, but this time, a sly, friendly grin accompanied Wanda's pet name for Skye.

"Sure," Skye said. "Do you want to keep shooting?"

"Nah." Wanda leaned her cue stick against the wall and strolled to her bed. "I just wanna talk." Instead of flopping into her usual pose, she sat on the edge of the futon and wrung her hands.

Wow, Skye thought. *She just wants to talk. This could be a biggie.* Skye parked her stick on the cue rack and sat next to Wanda. "So, Wanda, how'd you do on the report you wrote about pool for that English assignment?"

"The woman, I mean Mrs. C., gave me a 'C,'" Wanda chuckled. "How about that? A 'C' from Mrs. C. That's the best grade I ever got on an English paper."

"That's super," Skye said, then asked, "What's on your mind, Wanda?" She slid back and leaned against the wall, stretching her legs across the width of the futon.

Wanda looked down and for a moment and said nothing. Skye simply waited.

"Do you ever have bad dreams?" Wanda finally asked without looking at Skye.

"I did when I first moved in here. They were awful."

"Do you remember what they were about?" Wanda asked.

"Afraid so. Most of them were about me looking for my parents. In every dream, I searched and searched for them. I would see them off in the distance coming toward me, and just when I'd get close enough to see their faces, they'd turn and walk the other way. I could never catch them, no matter how fast I ran. I often woke up yelling and sweating like a grunting pig in a sauna."

"How come you don't get them anymore?"

"I think they stopped after I started listening to Mom's counsel about my being so mad at the whole wide world. I also accepted Christ into my life."

"How'd that help?" Wanda's question was sincere.

"Well, Christ gave me the strength to face my problems and stop running from them. Mom also showed me a verse in the Bible that helped me. That verse in Second Corinthians is one of my favorites: 'If anyone is in Christ he is a new creation; the old has gone, the new has come.'"

Wanda looked at Skye and shriveled up her face in a question mark. "What does that mean?"

"It means that when you ask Christ to forgive your sins and come into your life, you become a brand-new person from the inside out. He really did change me, Wanda. I think completely different now than I did before I accepted him into my life. You should try it."

"Yeah, Mrs. C. has been talking to me about that, but I'm not sure it will do me any good."

"After I became a Christian, I was able to forgive my parents for leaving me. I didn't even know them, but I hated them. I still don't have a clue who they are—or where they are, and that hurts. I've also been in over a dozen foster homes, and I've had a lot of baggage to deal with. Let me tell you, juvie hall was better than some of those foster homes."

"I ain't never been in no foster homes." Wanda went back to staring at the floor. "But the Blades were the only family I ever had. I've been running with them since I was about eight. That's when Mom died."

"What happened?"

Wanda brushed her cheek, wiping away a tear. "She had a heart attack."

"Wow," Skye said, "she mustn't have been very old."

"She was only thirty-two. Bad hearts run in the family." Wanda sniffled and wiped the back of her hand across her nose. "That's what's wrong with Gram too. She's always sick."

"What about your dad?"

"He's in jail. He'll be there about ten more years."

Skye was dying to know what the man had done, but she figured Wanda would tell her in her own good time. "What are your dreams about?"

"What dreams?" Wanda looked at Skye quickly.

"Wanda, I can hear you yelling. Your bed is right underneath my bedroom."

"I thought Mrs. C. was the only one who knew."

"Well, I know because I can hear you yelling," Skye assured her. "What are they about?"

Wanda just sat wringing her hands.

Skye slid right next to Wanda. "That's okay if you don't want to tell me. Maybe another time."

"No, I want to, but it's hard. I ain't never told nobody about them, about a lot of stuff."

"I'm all ears," Skye said. "And no one else will know unless you want me to tell."

"It's not that," Wanda said. "I just need to get enough guts to spill my guts."

"Can't you tell Mom?"

"I want to. I just can't yet," Wanda said.

Skye sat, waiting.

Without another word, Wanda lifted her sweatshirt, exposing her back.

Skye studied Wanda's back, and what she saw made her mouth drop open.

chapter sixteen

On Wanda's back were six round red scars, each about the size of a dime.

"Oh, Wanda!" was all Skye could say.

"There are more on my legs, too." Wanda put her sweatshirt back in place. Her beautiful brown eyes flooding with tears, she looked at Skye.

"How did you get those scars?" Skye felt her own eyes grow moist, and tears blurred her vision.

"They're ... they're ... cigarette burns."

"Was that some kind of initiation into the Blades, or what?"

Wanda glanced away, tears streaming down her cheeks and dropping freely unto the bed. "They're from my father," she cried. "That's why he's in jail, and I hate him."

Skye wasn't sure what was worse, having a parent who did something like that or not having any at all. All she knew at the moment was that she felt awfully bad for Wanda and desperately wanted to help her. *But how?*

Wanda sniffled and struggled to speak again. "Mom died a few weeks after they took my father away. Maybe she died of a broken heart. How's that for major heart trouble?"

"Wanda, I'm so sorry," Skye said. "I know you're hurting, and there's only one person who can help you get through this."

"Who?" Again with tear filled eyes, Wanda looked at Skye.

"God," Skye said. "I'm telling you that he's there for you. All you need to do is ask."

"I'll think about it," Wanda said with a forced smile.

"That's cool," Skye said. "And if I can help you with anything, just ask me, too. I really want to be your friend."

"Got it," Wanda sniffled. "And Skye?"

"Yep?"

"Thanks. Thanks a lot."

"No problem," Skye said, smiling.

Friday evening at the Chambers' supper table, the chatter was filled with excitement about the picnic the next afternoon. The weather report predicted a perfect first day of June with blue skies, warm sun, and a gentle breeze.

In charge of the menu, Morgan had found some new recipes for barbecued chicken sauce and toppings for baked potatoes. Skye had been helping Mr. Chambers groom the horses and polish the tack so that the horse part of the activities would be raring to go. Mrs. Chambers and Wanda were busy making the two bathrooms in the house and the restroom in the barn presentable for the day of the teen invasion. But the highlight of the discussion centered around Wanda.

Mrs. Chambers had the biggest smile on her face that Skye had seen in quite a long time. "Wanda, would you like to tell the family what happened during counseling this afternoon?"

Nibbling on a chip, Wanda looked like a bashful child who had just been praised for a job well done. Her dark brown eyes glanced at everyone while they stared, waiting.

"Well, Wanda," Mr. Chambers wiped his mustache with a napkin, "what's the great news? Don't keep us in such suspense."

"Yeah," Morgan added. "I'm always ready for some good news."

Wanda glanced at Skye and when their eyes met, Wanda's whole face lit up with a smile, something that Skye was sure she had *never* seen before.

"I'm on the edge of my seat, and I'm about to fall off," Skye joked. "C'mon, tell us."

"I accepted Christ as my Savior at Maranatha this afternoon," Wanda said, sheepishly.

"You did?" Mr. Chambers said.

"She did!" Mrs. Chambers proclaimed.

"Wow, that's awesome," Morgan said.

Beaming her own smile, Skye simply nodded at Wanda and gave her a thumbs-up.

Mrs. Chambers sipped a cup of coffee. "Wanda has come to grips with a lot of things in her life these past few weeks. I think she's starting to see how God can help her with all of her problems."

"Well, that's great," Mr. Chambers said. He relaxed into his chair and folded his arms. "This is the best news I've heard since our rebel Mustang got himself straightened out. Wanda, we've all been praying that you'd allow God to work in your heart. What made you decide to accept Christ?"

"It was something Skye said to me earlier this week when we were shooting pool and talking. She said God could help me not hate my father. Mrs. C. had told me that too, but I guess it's just starting to sink into this rock on my shoulders." Wanda tapped her head with her index finger. "I also saw how all you guys are so happy all the time. Even when you've got problems, you don't wanna go and throw yourself off a cliff. You're different from anybody else I know. I figured that's because you all have God in your life. I have a long way to go, but I think I'm on the right track."

"God will help you with all your problems," Morgan said. "You'll see."

"That's what I've been hearing," Wanda said and nibbled on another chip. "But there's one problem that I think *Skye* can help me with right this minute."

"Oh?" Mrs. Chambers said while everyone raised their eyebrows. "What's that?"

Again, Wanda glanced around the table and focused on Skye. "I'd like her to show me how to dress and act like a Christian girl."

"I wanna look real nice today 'cause I wanna tell everybody that I have Jesus in my life," Wanda said as she sat at Skye's dresser and stared at the mirror.

"You're off to a good start," Skye said, bending over Wanda and glancing at the mirror, too. "Now, with your new spike job with just the right mousse, your just-the-right make-up, and just-the-right threads, you'll make a grand entrance at the picnic today."

"What time are the church kids coming?" Wanda asked.

Skye glanced at her watch. "They're supposed to come at four o'clock."

"Skye," Wanda said as she stared at her own reflection, "Chad's not your boyfriend, is he?"

I sure hope someday, Skye thought as she stood next to Wanda and played with some tangled necklaces in her jewelry box. "Ah, no. We're too young to date," Skye said with some hesitation. "But we're real good friends. Why?"

"I'd like him to be my boyfriend," Wanda said. "Will you help me?"

You have got to be kidding. Skye felt her face flush, and her brain had no idea what to tell her lips to say next. "Ah—ah—" Skye stammered, "Mom and Dad won't allow any of us, even Morgan, to have boyfriends. We're all too young yet."

"Oh!" Wanda seemed startled. "My boyfriend, Wheels—you know from the gang?—we were a number for a couple of years. But he's been sent up, so as far as I'm concerned, we're history. He was no good for me anyway. Chad would be good for me."

Skye felt her heart nosedive into the pit of her stomach, and she thought she was going to be sick. *Chad and Wanda together?* "Well, I know Mom and Dad won't let you date Chad or anybody."

"Hmm." Wanda stared at the mirror. "At least I can let him know I'm interested for when we *are* older. I want to look so pretty today that I'll knock his socks off when he sees me."

I'd like to knock your block off right now, Skye grumbled and then gave herself a lecture. *Stop it. He's not interested in any girl, and he won't be interested in Wanda either.* Skye refocused and went back to the task. "Wanda, I'm thinking about how nice you looked in that pink blouse you wore awhile back. I believe pink is your color."

"I can wear that blouse today," Wanda said.

"Nah, that's too fancy for a picnic," Skye said. "Do you have any other kind of pink top?"

Wanda sat a moment, thinking. "I know. I have a pink pullover with short sleeves. That should be just right for today."

Skye held up a small gold heart necklace with one small rhinestone in the middle. "And if you wear a touch of jewelry to complete your new look, you should knock everyone's socks off." *Minus Chad's*, Skye determined.

At four o'clock sharp, the church bus rolled in to the Keystone Stables parking lot, and about a dozen teens and Mr. and Mrs. Salem, the chaperones, piled off.

Mr. Chambers and Skye had five horses tacked and lined up at the fence in the pasture, ready to go. Although Rebel had been doing fine with his training, Mr. Chambers decided that a dozen rambunctious teens might be just a little too much, so Rebel got the day off just watching the action from the training corral. Mrs. Chambers, Morgan, and Wanda were busy at the picnic grounds getting the grille going and setting the tables. At the house, the game room door had been propped opened, inviting all to partake in the fun that waited inside.

Skye stood petting Champ's neck and studying the bus as it emptied. As soon as she saw Chad, her heart did a double flip, and she yelled out to him.

"Chad, over here!" She waved and Chad looked her way.

"Be there in a sec, Skye!" he yelled. Then Skye noticed Chad saying something to a boy standing right next to him. Skye didn't know the other boy.

Chad and the boy, along with five girls, headed toward the pasture where Skye and Mr. Chambers waited with the horses. The chaperones and other teens headed toward the pavilion.

"Step right this way, ladies," Mr. Chambers said to the girls who approached the fence with a round of giggles.

"Can we ride now?" one asked.

"Sure," Mr. Chambers said. "Slip in through the rails and we'll get you mounted. You can ride in here." He pointed his thumb over his shoulder.

When one of the girls climbed on Champ, Skye gave her a crash course in riding and loosed the horse's reins from the fence. After all the girls had mounted, Mr. Chambers walked to the center of the field and threw out instructions to the girls who started to ride in a large circle around him.

Skye then turned her attention to Chad and the new boy. "Hi, Chad," Skye said.

"What's up, Skye?" Chad said. "I want you to meet Pete Gellito. He just moved here from Pittsburgh. He started working part-time at Culp's. That's where we met. Pete, this is Skye Nicholson. She lives here at Keystone Stables."

"Hel-lo, Skye Nicholson!" Pete immediately shifted his charm into overdrive.

"Hi, Pete!" *Whoa!* The young man had the blackest, waviest hair Skye had ever seen. His dark eyes set off a handsome face with a defined nose and square jaw. He reminded Skye of a picture of a Roman statue in her history book. *Not as cute as Chad*, Skye determined, *but close. Awfully close.* "How come you moved to these parts?" she asked Pete.

"My dad's corporation downsized, so he had a choice. He could either move to the satellite company here or lose his job. Big choice, huh?"

"I think you'll like it here in central PA," Chad said. "There's lots to do, and lots of nice kids to do them with." He winked at Skye, and her heart took off.

"I'm finding that out already," Pete said, staring at Skye. "The girls in this part of the country are something else."

Skye felt her face flush as she stared back into Chad's eyes.

"I want to show Pete around," Chad said. "I think we'll—"

"Hey, Chad ole' buddy! How are ya?" Wanda came charging across the lawn like a runaway train and slapped Chad on the shoulder. "Are you ready for a game of pool?"

Indeed, Wanda did make a striking appearance with her Skye-directed makeover, her pink top and delicate gold necklace. One thing Skye realized immediately was that she had failed to tell Wanda how to "talk" to boys. But with Chad in the center of the picture, Skye wasn't sure she was ready to do that. *I'd rather have Wanda be Chad's "ole' buddy" than his girlfriend*, she reasoned.

"Hi, Wanda," Chad said. "This is Pete Gellito. He just moved here from Pittsburgh. Pete, this is Wanda Stallord. She's a foster kid from Harrisburg. She stays here at Keystone Stables."

"Well, hel-lo, Wanda Stallord!" Pete said. "Where have you been all my life?"

"Double whoa!" Wanda parked her hands on her hips and studied Pete from head to toe. "Pittsburgh's loss, our gain. What grade are you in, hotshot?"

"I'm in tenth." Pete gave Wanda the once-over and seemed as though he thoroughly enjoyed her attention.

"I'm in eighth," Wanda chimed and never looked away from Pete. "But I'm homeschooling right now." In her next breath, she said, "I just accepted Jesus into my life. Are you a Christian, Pete?"

"Well, I go to church," Pete said.

"Not good enough," Wanda informed him. "You need Jesus in your life. I'll tell you about it later."

"I'd like to hear what you have to say," Pete said sincerely.

This is very good, Skye thought.

Chad tried to get a word in. "I'd like to show Pete around and—"

"So, Pete, have you ever shot pool?" Wanda interrupted.

"Pool's my game!" Pete said. "I even have my own cue stick. I was in a junior billiard league back home. Chad told me you had a pool table here, and I would have brought my cue, but it's still packed somewhere in a box at our new house. Guaranteed, the next time I come here, I'll have it with me."

This is super good! Skye thought as she and Chad exchanged smiles. "The pool table is just sitting in there waiting for us," Skye announced. "Why don't we make it a foursome?"

"Sounds like a plan," Chad said, glancing at his watch. "We have time for a few games before supper."

Wanda grabbed Pete by the arm and turned him toward the open door of the game room. "Well, hotshot, let's see if you can put your money where your mouth is. Nine Ball's my game."

"That's my game, too." Pete released a hearty laugh. "Double or nothing, ball in hand on a foul, gorgeous."

As Wanda and Pete headed across the lawn, Chad and Skye started to follow a short distance behind. Skye glanced back at the field to make sure Champ was in good hands. He was. Her gaze drifted to the training corral where Rebel stood with his neck arched out over the fence as he watched the other horses. Skye took an extra long look at the horse that had caused her so much trouble, but now he looked like he was almost smiling.

"Skye, ole' buddy..." Chad's words brought Skye back to his dimpled smile as he gently slapped her shoulder in mock-Wanda style. "It looks like we're going to have a great time here today."

"Chad, ole' buddy ..." Skye beamed her most radiant smile at one of her best friends in the whole wide world. "... I'm already having the greatest time of my life."

A Letter to my Keystone Stables Fans

Dear Reader,

Are you crazy about horses like I am? Are you fortunate enough to have a horse now, or are you dreaming about the day when you will have one of your very own?

I've been crazy about horses ever since I can remember. When I was a child, I lived where I couldn't have a horse. Even if I had lived in the country, my folks didn't have the money to buy me a horse. So, as I grew up in a small coal town in central Pennsylvania, I dreamed about horses and collected horse pictures and horse models. I drew horse pictures and wrote horse stories, and I read every horse book I could get my hands on.

For Christmas when I was ten, I received a leather-fringed western jacket and a cowgirl hat. Weather permitting, I wore them when I walked to and from school. On the way, I imagined that I was riding a gleaming white steed into a world of mountain trails and forest paths.

Occasionally, during the summer, my mother took me to a riding academy where I rode a horse for one hour at a time. I always rubbed my hands (and hard!) on my mount before we left the ranch. For the rest of the day I tried not to wash my hands so I could smell the horse and remember the great time I had. Of course, I never could sit at the dinner table without Mother first sending me to the faucet to get rid of that "awful stench."

To get my own horse, I had to wait until I grew up, married, and bought a home in the country with enough land for a barn and a pasture. Moon Doggie, my very first horse, was a handsome brown and white pinto Welsh Mountain Pony. Many other equines came to live at our place where, in later years, my husband and I also opened our hearts to foster kids who needed a caring home. Most of the kids loved the horses as much as I did.

Although owning horses and rearing foster kids are now in my past, I fondly remember my favorite steed, who has long since passed from the scene. Rex, part Quarter Horse and part Tennessee Walker, was a 14 ½ hands-high bay. Rex was the kind of horse every kid dreams about. With a smooth walking gait, he gave me a thrilling ride every time I climbed into the saddle. Yet, he was so gentle, a young child could sit confidently on his back. Rex loved sugar cubes and nuzzled my pockets to find them. When cleaning his hooves, all I had to do was touch the target leg, and he lifted his hoof into my waiting hands. Rex was my special horse, and although he died at the ripe old age of twenty-five many years ago, I still miss him.

If you have a horse now or just dream about the day when you will, I beg you to do all you can to learn how to treat with tender love and respect one of God's most beautiful creatures. Horses make wonderful pets, but they require much more attention than a dog or a cat. For their loyal devotion to you, they only ask that you love them in return with the proper food, a clean barn, and the best of care.

Rex

Although Skye's and Wanda's story that you just read is fiction, the following pages contain horse facts that any horse lover will enjoy. It is my desire that these pages will help you to either care for your own horse better now or prepare you for that moment when you'll be able to throw your arms around that one special horse of your dreams that you can call your very own.

Happy riding!
Marsha Hubler

Are You Ready to Own Your First Horse?

The most exciting moment in any horse lover's life is to look into the eyes of a horse she can call her very own. No matter how old you are when you buy your first horse, it's hard to match the thrill of climbing onto his back and taking that first ride on a woodsy trail or dusty road that winds through open fields. A well-trained mount will give you a special friendship and years of pleasure as you learn to work with him and become a confident equestrian team.

But owning a horse involves much more than hopping on his back, racing him into a lather of sweat, and putting him back in his stall until you're ready to ride him again.

If you have your own horse now, you've already realized that caring for a horse takes a great amount of time and money. Besides feeding him twice a day, you must also groom him, clean his stall, "pick" his hooves, and have a farrier (a horseshoe maker and applier) and veterinarian make regular visits.

If you don't own a horse and you are begging your parents to buy one, please realize that you can't keep the horse in your garage and just feed him grass cuttings left over from a mowed lawn. It is a sad fact that too many neglected horses have ended up in rescue shelters after well-meaning families did not know how to properly care for their steeds.

If you feel that you are ready to have your own horse, please take time to answer the following questions. If you say yes to all of them, then you are well on your way to being the proud owner of your very own mount.

1. Do you have the money to purchase:

   - the horse? (A good grade horse can start at $800. Registered breeds can run into the thousands.)
   - a saddle, pad, and bridle, and a winter blanket or raincoat? ($300+ brand new)
   - a hard hat (helmet) and riding boots? ($150+)
   - essentials such as coat and hoof conditioner, bug repellent, electric clipper and grooming kit, saddle soap, First Aid kit, and vitamins? ($150+)

2. Does your family own at least a one-stall shed or barn and at least two acres of grass (enough pasture for one horse) to provide adequate grazing for your horse during warm months? If not, do you have the money to regularly purchase quality oats and alfalfa/timothy hay, and do you have the place to store the hay? Oh, and let's not forget the constant supply of sawdust or straw you need for stall bedding!

3. Are you ready to get up early enough every day to give your horse a bucket of fresh water, feed him a coffee can full of oats and one or two sections of clean dry hay (if you have no pasture), and "muck out" the manure from the barn?

4. Every evening, are you again ready to water and feed your horse, clean the barn, groom him, and pick his hooves?
5. Will you ride him at least twice a week, weather permitting?
6. If the answer to any of the above questions is no, then does your family have the money to purchase a horse and board him at a nearby stable? (Boarding fees can run as high as a car payment. Ask your parents how much that is.)

So, there you have the bare facts about owning and caring for a horse. If you don't have your own horse yet, perhaps you'll do as I did when I was young: I read all the books I could about horses. I analyzed all the facts about the money and care needed to make a horse happy. Sad as it made me feel, I finally realized that I would have to wait until I was much older to assume such a great responsibility. And now years later, I can look back and say, "For the horse's sake, I'm very glad I did wait."

I hope you've made the decision to give your horse the best possible TLC that you can. That might mean improving his care now or waiting until you're older to get a horse of your own. Whatever you and your parents decide, please remember that the result of your efforts should be a happy horse. If that's the case, you will be happy too.

Let's Go Horse Shopping!

If you are like I was when I was younger, I dreamed of owning the most beautiful horse in the world. My dream horse, with his long-flowing mane and wavy tail dragging on the ground, would arch his neck and prance with only a touch of my hand on his withers or a gentle rub of my boot heel on his barrel. My dream horse was often different colors. Sometimes he was silvery white; other times he was jet black. He was often a pinto blend of the deepest chocolate browns, blacks, and whites. No matter what color he was, he always took me on a perfect ride, responding to my slightest commands.

When I was old enough to be responsible to care for my own steed, I already knew that the horse of my dreams was just that, the horse of my dreams. To own a prancing pure white stallion or a high-stepping coal-black mare, I would have to buy a Lipizzaner, American Saddle Horse, or an Andalusian. But those kinds of horses were either not for sale to a beginner with a tiny barn or they cost so much, I couldn't afford one. I was amazed to discover that there are about 350 different breeds of horses, and I had to look for a horse that was just right for me, possibly even a good grade horse (that means not registered) that was a safe mount. Color really didn't matter as long as the horse was healthy and gave a safe, comfortable ride. (But I'm not sure what my friends might have said if I had a purple horse. That certainly would have been a "horse of a different color!") Then I had to decide if I wanted to ride western or English style. Well, living in central Pennsylvania farm country with oodles of trails and dirt roads, the choice for me was simple: western.

I'm sure if you don't have your own horse yet, you've dreamed and thought a lot about what your first horse will be. Perhaps you've already had a horse, but now you're thinking of buying another one. What kind should you get?

Let's look at some of the breeds that are the most popular for both western and English riders today. We'll briefly trace a few breeds' roots and characteristics while you decide if that kind of horse might be the one for you. Please keep in mind that this information speaks to generalities of the breeds. If given the proper care and training, most any breeds of horses make excellent mounts as well.

Some Popular Breeds (Based on Body Confirmation)

The Arabian

Sometimes called "The China Doll of the Horse Kingdom," the Arabian is known as the most beautiful of horse breeds because of its delicate features. Although research indicates Arabians are the world's oldest and purest breed, it is not known whether they originated in Arabia. However, many Bible scholars believe that the first horse that God created in the Garden of Eden must have embodied the strength and beauty that we see in the Arabian horse of today. It is also believed that all other breeds descended from this gorgeous breed that has stamina as well as courage and intelligence.

A purebred Arabian has a height of only 14 or 15 hands, a graceful arch in his neck, and a high carriage in his tail. It is easy to identify one of these horses by examining his head. If you see a small, delicate "dish" face with a broad forehead and tiny muzzle, two ears that point inward and large eyes that are often ringed in black, you are probably looking at an Arabian. The breed comes in all colors, (including dappled and some paint), but if you run your finger against the grain of any pureblood Arabian's coat, you will see an underlying bed of black skin. Perhaps that's why whites are often called "grays."

Generally, Arabians are labeled spirited and skittish, even though they might have been well trained. If you have your heart set on buying an Arabian, make sure you first have the experience to handle a horse that, although he might be loyal, will also want to run with the wind.

The Morgan

The Morgan Horse, like a Quarter Horse (see below), can explode into a gallop for a short distance. The Morgan, with its short legs, muscles, and fox ears, also looks very much like the Quarter Horse. How can we tell the two breeds apart?

127

A Morgan is chunkier than a Quarter Horse, especially in his stout neck. His long, wavy tail often flows to the ground. His trot is quick and short and with such great stamina, he can trot all day long.

So where are the Morgan's roots?

The horse breed was named after Justin Morgan, a frail music teacher who lived in Vermont at the turn of the eighteenth century. Instead of receiving cash for a debt owed, Mr. Morgan was given two colts. The smallest one, which he called Figure, was an undersized dark bay with a black mane and tail. Mr. Morgan sold the one colt, but he kept Figure, which he thought was a cross between a Thoroughbred and an Arabian. Over the years, he found the horse to be strong enough to pull logs and fast enough to beat Thoroughbreds in one afternoon and eager to do it all over again the same day!

When Mr. Morgan died, his short but powerful horse was called "Justin Morgan" in honor of his owner. After that, all of Justin Morgan's foals were called Morgans. The first volume of the Morgan Horse Register was published in 1894. Since then, hundreds of thousands of Morgans have been registered.

If you go Morgan hunting, you will find the breed in any combination of blacks, browns, and whites. Don't look for a tall horse because all Morgans are between 14 and 15 hands tall, just right for beginners. If you're fortunate enough to find a well-trained Morgan, he'll give you years of pleasure whether you ask him to gallop down a country trail, pull a wagon, or learn to jump obstacles.

The Mustang

If you want a taste of America's Wild West from days gone by, then you should treat yourself to the "Wild Horse of America," the Mustang.

This 14–15 hand, stout horse has its roots from Cortez and the Spanish conquistadors from the sixteenth century. Although the Mustang's name comes from the Spanish word, *mesteno*, which means "a stray or wild grazer," he is most well known as the horse of the Native Americans. Numerous tribes all over the western plains captured horses that had escaped from their Spanish owners and ran wild. The Native Americans immediately claimed the Mustang as a gift from their gods and showed the world that the horse was, and is, easy to train once domesticated.

It didn't take long for the white settlers to discover the versatility of the Mustang. Because of his endurance, this little horse soon became a favorite for the Pony Express, the U.S. cavalry, cattle round-ups, and caravans.

Since the 1970s, the U.S. Bureau of Land Management has stepped in to save the Mustangs from extinction. As a result, herds of Mustangs still roam freely in U.S. western plains today. At different times of the year and in different parts of the country, the Adopt-a-Horse-or-Burro Program allows horse lovers to take a Mustang or burro home for a year and train it to be a reliable mount. After the year, the eligible family can receive a permanent ownership title from the government. As of October 2007, more than 218,000 wild horses and burros have been placed into private care since the adoption program began in 1973.

If you'd like a "different" kind of horse that sometimes has a scrubby look but performs with the fire of the Arab-barb blood, then go shopping for a Mustang. You'll find him in any black, brown, or white combination and with the determination and stamina to become your best equine friend.

The Quarter Horse

There's no horse lover anywhere in the world who hasn't heard of the American Quarter Horse. In fact, the Quarter Horse is probably the most popular breed in the United States today.

But what exactly is a Quarter Horse? Is he only a quarter of a horse in size, therefore, just a pony? No, this fantastic breed isn't a quarter of anything!

The Quarter Horse originated in American colonial times in Virginia when European settlers bred their stout English workhorses with the Native Americans' Mustangs. The result? A short-legged but muscular equine with a broad head and little "fox" ears, a horse that has great strength and speed.

It didn't take long for the colonists and Native Americans to discover that their new crossbreed was the fastest piece of horseflesh in the world for a quarter of a mile. Thus, the breed was christened the American Quarter Horse and began to flourish. Besides running quick races, it also pulled wagons, canal boats, and plows. When the American West opened up, cowpokes discovered that the Quarter Horse was perfect for herding cattle and to help rope steers. Although it remained a distinct breed for over three hundred years in the U.S., the Quarter Horse was only recognized with its own studbook in 1941.

If you are looking for a reliable mount that has a comfortable trot and smooth gallop, you might want to look at some *seasoned* Quarter Horses. (That means they have been trained properly and are at least five or six years old.) They come in any color or combination of colors. Their temperament is generally friendly, yet determined to get the job done that you ask them to do.

The Shetland Pony

Many beginning riders incorrectly believe that the smaller the horse, the easier it is to control him. You might be thinking, "I'm tiny, so I need a tiny horse!" But many beginners have found out the hard way that a Shetland Pony is sometimes no piece of cake.

Shetland Ponies originated as far back as the Bronze Age in the Shetland Isles, northeast of mainland Scotland.

Research has found that they are related to the ancient Scandinavian ponies. Shetland Ponies were first used for pulling carts, carrying peat and other items, and plowing farmland. Thousands of Shetlands also worked as "pit ponies," pulling coal carts in British mines in the mid–nineteenth century. The Shetland found its way at the same time to the United States when they were imported to also work in mines.

The American Shetland Pony Club was founded in 1888 as a registry to keep the pedigrees for all the Shetlands that were being imported from Europe at that time.

Shetlands are usually only 10.2 hands or shorter. They have a small head, sometimes with a dished face, big Bambi eyes, and small ears. The original breed has a short, muscular neck, stocky bodies, and short, strong legs. Shetlands can give you a bouncy ride because of their short broad backs and deep girths. These ponies have long thick manes and tails, and in winter climates their coats of any color can grow long and fuzzy.

If you decide you'd like to own a Shetland, spend a great deal of time looking for one that is mild mannered. Because of past years of hard labor, the breed now shows a dogged determination that often translates into stubbornness. So be careful, and don't fall for that sweet, fuzzy face without riding the pony several times before you buy him. You might get a wild, crazy ride from a "shortstuff" mount that you never bargained for!

The Tennessee Walking Horse

If you buy a Tennessee Walker, get ready for a thrilling ride as smooth as running water!

The Tennessee Walking Horse finds its roots in 1886 in Tennessee, when a Standardbred (a Morgan and Standardbred trotter cross) stallion named Black Allan refused to trot; instead, he chose to amble or "walk" fast. With effortless speed comparable to other horses' trots,

Black Allan's new gait (each hoof hitting the ground at a different time) amazed the horse world. Owners of Thoroughbreds and saddle horses were quick to breed their mares to this delightful new "rocking-horse" stud, and the Tennessee Walker was on its way to becoming one of the most popular breeds in the world. In just a few short years, the Walker became the favorite mount of not only circuit-riding preachers and plantation owners, but ladies riding sidesaddle as well.

Today the Walker, which comes in any black, brown, or white color or combination, is a versatile horse and is comfortable when ridden English or Western. He is usually 15 to 17 hands tall and has a long neck and sloping shoulders. His head is large but refined, and he has small ears. Because he has a short back, his running walk, for which he is known, comes naturally.

If you go shopping for a Tennesee Walker, you will find a horse that is usually mild mannered yet raring to go. Although most Walkers are big and you might need a stepstool to climb on one, you will be amazed at how smooth his walk and rocking-horse canter is. In fact, you might have trouble making yourself get off!

Some Popular Breeds (Based on Body Color)

The Appaloosa

French cave paintings thousands of years old have "spotted" horses among its subjects, ancient China had labeled their spotted horses as "heavenly," and Persians have called their spotted steeds "sacred." Yet the spotted Appaloosa breed that we know today is believed to have originated in the northwestern Native Americans tribe called the Nez Perce in the seventeenth century.

When colonists expanded the United States territory westward, they found a unique people who lived near the Palouse River (which runs from north central Idaho to the Snake River in southeast Washington State). The Nez Perce Indian tribe had bred a unique horse—red or blue roans with white spots on the rump. Fascinated, the colonists called the beautiful breed *palousey*, which means "the stream of the green meadows." Gradually, the name changed to *Appaloosa*.

The Nez Perce people lost most of their horses following the end of the Nez Perce War in 1877, and the breed started to decline for several decades. However, a small number of dedicated Appaloosa lovers kept the breed alive. Finally, a breed registry was formed in 1938. The Appaloosa was named the official state horse of Idaho in 1975.

If you decide to buy an Appaloosa, you'll own one of the most popular breeds in the United States today. It is best known as a stock horse used in a number of western riding events, but it's also seen in many other types of equestrian contests as well. So if you would like to ride English or Western, or want to show your horse or ride him on a mountain trail, an Appaloosa could be just the horse for you.

Appaloosas can be any solid base color, but the gorgeous blanket of spots that sometimes cover the entire horse identifies the special breed. Those spotted markings are not the same as pintos or the "dapple grays" and some other horse colors. For a horse to be registered as a pureblood Appaloosa, it also has to have striped hooves, white outer coat (sclera) encircling its brown or blue eyes, and mottled (spotted) skin around the eyes and lips. The Appaloosa is one of the few breeds to have skin mottling, and so this characteristic is a surefire way of identifying a true member of the breed.

In 1983, the Appaloosa Horse Club in America decided to limit the crossbreeding of Appaloosas to only three main confirmation breeds: the Arabian, the American Quarter Horse, and the Thoroughbred. Thus, the Appaloosa color breed also became a true confirmation breed as well.

If you want your neighbors to turn their heads your way when you ride past, then look for a well-trained Appaloosa. Most registered "Apps" are 15 hands or shorter but are full of muscle and loaded with spots. Sometimes, though, it takes several years for an Appaloosa's coat to mature to its full color. So if it's color you're looking for, shop for a seasoned App!

The Pinto

The American Pinto breed has its origins in the wild Mustang of the western plains. The seventeenth and eighteenth century Native Americans bred color into their "ponies," using them for warhorses and prizing those with the richest colors. When the "Westward Ho" pioneers captured wild Mustangs with flashy colors, they bred them to all different breeds of European stock horses. Thus, the Pinto has emerged as a color breed, which includes all different body shapes and sizes today.

The Pinto Horse Association of America was formed in 1956, although the bloodlines of many Pintos can be traced three or four generations before then. The association doesn't register Appaloosas, draft breeds, or horses with mule roots or characteristics. Today more than 100,000 Pintos are registered throughout the U.S., Canada, Europe, and Asia.

Pintos have a dark background with random patches of white and have two predominant color patterns:

1. Tobiano (Toe-bee-ah'-no) Pintos are white with large spots of brown or black color. Spots can cover much of the head, chest, flank, and rump, often including the tail. Legs are generally white, which makes the horse look like he's white with flowing spots of color. The white usually crosses the center of the back of the horse.

2. Overo (O-vair'-o) Pintos are colored horses with jagged white markings that originate on the animal's side or belly and spread toward the neck, tail, legs, and back. The deep, rich browns or blacks appear to frame the white. Thus, Overos often have dark backs and dark legs. Horses with bald or white faces are often Overos. Their splashy white markings on the rest of their body make round, lacy patterns.

Perhaps you've heard the term *paint* and wonder if that kind of horse is the same as a Pinto. Well, amazingly, the two are different breeds! A true Paint horse (registered by the American Paint Horse Association) must be bred from pureblood Paints, Quarter Horses, or Thoroughbreds. The difference in eligibility between the two registries has to do with the bloodlines of the horse, not its color or pattern.

So if you're shopping for a flashy mount and you don't care about a specific body type of horse, then set your sites on a Pinto or Paint. You might just find a well-trained registered or grade horse that has the crazy colors you've been dreaming about for a very long time!

The Palomino
No other color of horse will turn heads his way than the gorgeous golden Palomino. While the average person thinks the ideal color for a Palomino is like a shiny gold coin, the Palomino breed's registry allows all kinds of coat colors as long as the mane and tail are silvery white. A white blaze can be on the face but can't extend beyond the eyes. The Palomino can also have white stockings, but the white can't extend beyond the knees. Colors of Palominos can range from a deep, dark chocolate to an almost-white cremello. As far as body confirmation, four breeds are strongly represented in crossbreeding with the

Palomino today: the American Saddlebred, Tennessee Walker, Morgan, and Quarter Horse.

No one is sure where the Palomino came from, but it is believed that the horse came from Spain. An old legend says that Isabella, queen of Spain in the late fifteenth century, loved her golden horses so much she sent one stallion and five mares across the Atlantic to start thriving in the New World. Eventually those six horses lived in what is now Texas and New Mexico, where Native Americans captured the horses' offspring and incorporated them into their daily lives. From those six horses came all the Palominos in the United States, which proves how adaptable the breed is in different climates.

Today you can find Palominos all over the world and involved in all kinds of settings from jumping to ranching to rodeos. One of their most popular venues is pleasing crowds in parades, namely the Tournament of Roses Parade in Pasadena, California, every New Year's Day.

Perhaps you've dreamed of owning a horse that you could be proud of whether you are trail riding on a dirt road, showing in a western pleasure class, or strutting to the beat of a band in a parade. If that's the case, then the Palomino is the horse for you!

If you're shopping for the best in bloodlines, look for a horse that has a double registry! With papers that show the proper bloodlines, an Appaloosa Quarter Horse can be double registered. Perhaps you'd like a palomino Morgan or a pinto Tennessee Walker?

Who Can Ride a Horse?

As you have read this book about Skye, Morgan, and some of the other children with special needs, perhaps you could identify with one in particular. Do you have what society calls a handicap or disability? Do you use a wheelchair? Do you have any friends who are blind or have autism? Do you or your friends with special needs believe that none of you could ever ride a horse?

Although Keystone Stables is a fictitious place, there are real ranches and camps that connect horses with children just like Skye and Morgan, Sooze in book two, Tanya in book three, Jonathan in book four, Katie in book five, Joey in book six, and Wanda in book seven. That special kind of treatment and interaction has a long complicated name called Equine Facilitated Psychotherapy (EFP.)

EFP might include handling and grooming the horse, lunging, riding, or driving a horse-drawn cart. In an EFP program, a licensed mental health professional works together with a certified horse handler. Sometimes one EFP person can have the credentials for both. Whatever the case, the professionals are dedicated to helping both the child and the horse learn to work together as a team.

Children with autism benefit greatly because of therapeutic riding. Sometimes a child who has never been able to speak or "connect" with another person, even a parent, will bond with a horse in such a way that the child learns to relate to other people or starts to talk.

An author friend has told me of some of her family members who've had experience with horses and autistic children. They tell a story about a mute eight-year-old boy who was taking therapeutic treatment. One day as he was riding a well-trained mount that knew just what to do, the horse stopped for no reason and refused to budge. The leader said, "Walk on" and pulled on the halter, but the horse wouldn't move. The sidewalkers (people who help the child balance in the saddle) all did the same thing with the same result. Finally, the little boy who was still sitting on the horse shouted, "Walk on, Horsie!" The horse immediately obeyed.

So the good news for some horse-loving children who have serious health issues is that they might be able to work with horses. Many kids like Morgan, who has cerebral palsy, and blind Katie (book five) actually can learn to ride! That's because all over the world, people who love horses and children have started therapy riding academies to teach children with special needs how to ride and/or care for a horse. Highly trained horses and special equipment like high-backed saddles with Velcro strips on the fenders make it safe for kids with special needs to become skilled equestrians and thus learn to work with their own handicaps as they never have been able to do before!

A Word about Horse Whispering

If you are constantly reading about horses and know a lot about them, you probably have heard of horse whispering, something that many horse behaviorists do today to train horses. This training process is much different than what the majority of horsemen did several decades ago.

We've all read Wild West stories or seen movies in which the cowpoke "broke" a wild horse by climbing on his back and hanging on while the poor horse bucked until he was so exhausted he could hardly stand. What that type of training did was break the horse's spirit, and the horse learned to obey out of fear. Many "bronco busters" from the past also used whips, ropes, sharp spurs, and painful bits to make the horses respond, which they did only to avoid the pain the trainers caused.

Thankfully, the way many horses become reliable mounts has changed dramatically. Today many horses are trained, not broken. The trainer "communicates" with the horse using herd language. Thus, the horse bonds with his trainer quickly, looks to that person as his herd leader, and is ready to obey every command.

Thanks to Monty Roberts, the "man who listens to horses," and other professional horse whispering trainers like him, most raw or green horses (those that are just learning to respond to tack and a rider) are no longer broken.

Horses are now trained to accept the tack and rider in a short time with proven methods of horse whispering. Usually working in a round pen, the trainer begins by making large movements and noise as a predator would, encouraging the horse to run away. The trainer then gives the horse the choice to flee or bond. Through body language, the trainer asks the horse, "Will you choose me to be your herd leader and follow me?"

Often the horse responds with predictable herd behavior by twitching an ear toward his trainer then by lowering his head and licking to display an element of trust. The trainer mocks the horse's passive body language, turns his back on the horse, and, without eye contact, invites him to come closer. The bonding occurs when the horse chooses to be with the human and walks toward the trainer, thus accepting his leadership and protection.

Horse whispering has become one of the most acceptable, reliable, and humane ways to train horses. Today we have multitudes of rider-and-horse teams that have bonded in such a special way, both the rider and the horse enjoy each other's company. So when you're talking to your friends about horses, always remember to say the horses have been trained, not broken. The word *broken* is part of the horse's past and should remain there forever.

Bible Verses about Horses

Do you know there are about 150 verses in the Bible that include the word *horse*? It seems to me that if God mentioned horses so many times in the Bible, then he is very fond of one of his most beautiful creatures.

Some special verses about horses in the Bible make any horse lover want to shout. Look at this exciting passage from the book of Revelation that tells us about a wonderful time in the future:

"I saw heaven standing open and there before me was a white horse, whose rider is called Faithful and True. With justice he judges and makes war. His eyes are like blazing fire, and on his head are many crowns. He has a name written on him that no one knows but he himself. He is dressed in a robe dipped in blood, and his name is the Word of God. The armies of heaven were following him riding on white horses and dressed in fine linen, white and clean" (Revelation 19:11 – 14).

The rider who is faithful and true is the Lord Jesus Christ. The armies of heaven on white horses who follow Jesus are those who have accepted him as their Lord and Savior. I've accepted Christ, so I know that some day I'll get to ride a white horse in heaven. Do you think he will be a Lipizzaner, an Andalusian, or an Arabian? Maybe it will be a special new breed of white horses that God is preparing just for that special time.

Perhaps you never realized that there are horses in heaven. Perhaps you never thought about how you could go to heaven when you die. You can try to be as good as gold, but the Bible says that to go to heaven, you must ask Jesus to forgive your sins. Verses to think about: "For all have sinned and fall short of the glory of God" (Romans 3:23); "For God so loved the world that he gave his one and only son, that whoever believes in him shall not perish but have eternal life (John 3:16); "For everyone who calls on the name of the Lord will be saved" (Romans 10:13).

Do you want to be part of Jesus' cavalry in heaven some day? Have you ever asked Jesus to forgive your sins and make you ready for heaven? If you've never done so, please ask Jesus to save your soul today.

As I'm riding my prancing white steed with his long wavy mane and tail dragging to the ground, I'll be looking for you!

Glossary of Gaits

Gait – A gait is the manner of movement; the way a horse goes.

There are four natural or major gaits most horses use: walk, trot, canter, and gallop.

Walk – In the walk, the slowest gait, hooves strike the ground in a four-beat order: right hind hoof, right fore (or front) hoof, left hind hoof, left fore hoof.

Trot – In the trot, hooves strike the ground in diagonals in a one-two beat: right hind and left forefeet together, left hind and right forefeet together.

Canter – The canter is a three-beat gait containing an instant during which all four hooves are off the ground. The foreleg that lands last is called the *lead* leg and seems to point in the direction of the canter.

Gallop – The gallop is the fastest gait. If fast enough, it's a four-beat gait, with each hoof landing separately: right hind hoof, left hind hoof just before right fore hoof, left fore hoof.

Other gaits come naturally to certain breeds or are developed through careful breeding.

Running walk–This smooth gait comes naturally to the Tennessee Walking Horse. The horse glides between a walk and a trot.

Pace–A two-beat gait, similar to a trot. But instead of legs pairing in diagonals as in the trot, fore and hind legs on one side move together, giving a swaying action.

Slow gait–Four beats, but with swaying from side to side and a prancing effect. The slow gait is one of the gaits used by five-gaited saddle horses. Some call this pace the *stepping pace* or *amble*.

Amble–A slow, easy gait, much like the pace.

Rack–One of the five gaits of the five-gaited American Saddle Horse, it's a fancy, fast walk. This four-beat gait is faster than the trot and is very hard on the horse.

Jog–A jog is a slow trot, sometimes called a *dogtrot*.

Lope–A slow, easygoing canter, usually referring to a western gait on a horse ridden with loose reins.

Fox trot–An easy gait of short steps in which the horse basically walks in front and trots behind. It's a smooth gait, great for long-distance riding and characteristic of the Missouri Fox Trotter.

Parts of a Horse

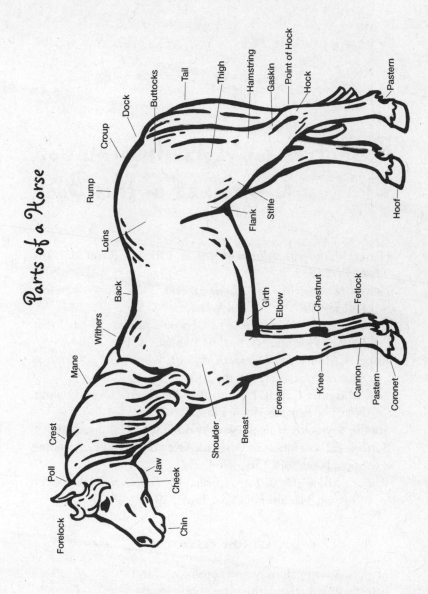

Poll, Crest, Mane, Withers, Back, Loins, Rump, Croup, Dock, Buttocks, Tail, Thigh, Hamstring, Gaskin, Point of Hock, Hock, Pastern, Flank, Stifle, Hoof, Forelock, Jaw, Cheek, Chin, Shoulder, Breast, Forearm, Girth, Elbow, Chestnut, Knee, Cannon, Pastern, Coronet, Fetlock

Resources for Horse Information Contained in this Book

Henry, Marguerite. *Album of Horses*. Chicago: Rand McNally & Co., 1952.

Henry, Marguerite. *All About Horses*. New York: Random House, 1967.

Jeffery, Laura. *Horses: How to Choose and Care for a Horse*. Berkley Heights, NJ: Enslow Publishers, Inc., 2004.

Roberts, Monty. *The Horses in My Life*. Pomfret, VT: Trafalgar Square Publishers, North, 2004.

Self, Margaret Cabell. *How to Buy the Right Horse*. Omaha, NE: The Farnam Horse Library, 1971.

Simon, Seymour. *Horses*. New York: HarperCollins, 2006.

Sutton, Felix. *Horses of America*. New York: G.P. Putnam's Sons, New York City, 1964.

Ulmer, Mike. *H is for Horse: An Equestrian Alphabet*. Chelsea, MI: Sleeping Bear Press, 2004.

Online resources

http://www.appaloosayouth.com/index.html
http://www.shetlandminiature.com/kids.asp
http://www.twhbea.com/youth/youthHome.aspx